The Secrets of the Cypress

Kari Alice

The Secrets of the Cypress

Edited by Dori Harrell

DoriHarrell.wix.com/BreakoutEditing

Cover by IndieDesignz.com

Formatting by Wild Seas Formatting

(http://www.WildSeasFormatting.com)

Published by Bay Isle Publishing

Text copyright © 2017 by Kari Alice

www.KariAlice.com

Subscribe to her mailing list.

For Sid and Dave, my parents. You both raised me to be the quirky dreamer I am today and have loved me no matter what. Mom, you always fed my stomach and were the voice of assurance and reason. You served as my voice when I was too shy to speak up for myself. Dad, you indulged my imagination by letting everything I created have value in your eyes. If a situation arose that seemed like too much for me to bear, you always let me know that it wasn't the end of the world. I wouldn't be the person I am today if not for you both.

For Jason, Kaylee, and Jemma–because I love you all so very much.

Chapter 1

Distraction

Libby

March arrived but was cold as a meat locker. My parka was my constant companion. As I drove to Shelby's, I shivered. My universe had tilted… Shelby, my best friend, was getting married. Today we'd meet up to begin our first official wedding preparations. So what if she'd ditched me by forgoing all our weekly lunches and shopping excursions. They didn't seem to matter to her, not when her every waking moment was centered on her groom-to-be, Danny.

I'd just finished decorating a doctor's house in Eden, Maryland, and had taken to keeping a box of wine in my refrigerator. I could go out with colleagues, but that was unlikely, as most were married part-timers with children. So as my social life trickled down the drain, I was caught in the cusp between the partying college life and children's playdates. Or, of course, jazzercise. I didn't resent Shelby for having it all, but the thought of being cooped up in the woods made me shudder. I just wanted my friend back…

I spotted Shelby's car in her parents' driveway and pulled in behind her. She'd asked me to be the maid of honor. Nothing had been booked yet, but the tentative date was set around Christmas. On one of my last visits here, I'd cried in front of both Shelby and her mom. If I could erase their memory of that, I would. My hormones had to be out of whack. Shelby's mom, Janice, was so sweet to me, but the pity that crinkled her nose still lingered in my memory. Why had I let a man get to me like that? It'd been so stupid.

I wore one of my brighter-colored dresses to dispel any remaining sympathy from that visit months ago. Today I had slipped into an A-line royal-blue dress with black trim. My hair was root-free, having been bleached a silvery platinum a few days ago. There'd be no doubt I'd regained my footing.

I let myself into the house, as the Camps were like my own family. As a teenager, I'd sometimes hung out with Janice, even when Shelby wasn't home.

"Come on in, Libby," Janice said as she gestured to a seat at the kitchen table, where Shelby was already sitting with her willowy arms resting on the table. Her hair rippled in waves that cascaded around the tops of her shoulders. She looked great, but somehow not quite right. I'd noticed it the last time I'd seen her too, but maybe she was happier now than she'd been in a long time. Her skin was flawless, like an airbrushed photograph, and she moved with grace that she'd never mastered until now. I needed to follow suit. Then maybe life would be effortless for me too.

I gave both Janice and Shelby a brief hug before sitting. Shelby's frail-looking body hid her durability. She was small but solid. "Oh my gosh, Shelby, you're so thin." I noted the hollows in her clavicles—she was far too skinny, no matter how solid she felt.

"I'm fine, Libby. Besides, I'm no smaller than you are." Shelby adjusted her sweater and pulled it down over her narrow hips, covered in tight-fitting leggings that revealed a wide thigh gap. *Who had a thigh gap? Geesh…*

"Can I get you something to drink?" Janice asked as she placed a basket of blueberry muffins on the table. She handed Shelby and me small plates.

"Do you have tea?" I wasn't thirsty, but I'd need something to wash down the mouth-watering muffin. I'd eat one even though I wasn't hungry.

Janice pulled a pitcher out of the refrigerator and poured a full glass of tea over ice.

"Thank you." I took a sip. The sugar content had to be off the charts.

"Certainly," Janice said. She grabbed several pamphlets from the countertop and sat down to join us at the kitchen table. Shelby sipped ice water but ignored the muffins. I couldn't see a bulge, so maybe she wasn't pregnant yet? That would explain the rushed engagement, but since the wedding was several months away, pregnancy couldn't be the reason, could it?

"So you can see that we have a lot to go through." Janice fanned the pamphlets in front of her.

"Have you settled on the date yet? You'll need one to reserve a venue," I said to Shelby. That was Party Planning 101. Her expression lacked its normal tentative quality, as if she were a strange and foreign being. What'd happened to the nervous Nellie I'd known? This Shelby acted self-assured and looked more beautiful than I'd admit. She'd donned a forest-green sweater and brown tights. The outfit wasn't bad per se, but it should've washed out her pale skin. But no, she almost glowed.

"We were thinking December thirtieth? It'd be after Christmas and would still give our guests time to celebrate New Year's." Shelby gaze settled on me, and for a moment I lost track of my thoughts.

"O-okay," I stammered as I accessed the calendar on my phone. I blinked a few times to regain focus.

"I'll check to see if the church is free for—"

Shelby cut her mom off midsentence. "Actually, we wanted to have the wedding someplace else." Shelby flicked her eyes at me before turning back to her mom.

Janice's brows knitted together, as if this wasn't up for discussion. "You know how I feel about church weddings."

We all knew how she felt about church weddings.

"I know, Mom, but Danny and I've talked about it. We want something different." Shelby shifted in her seat, but she didn't seem upset by her mother's reaction. Her expression remained placid as pond water.

"Then where?" Janice asked as she scattered the pile of pamphlets from the table. Some of the pamphlets fell to the floor, but no one bent down to pick them up.

I'd bolt from the room if I could go unnoticed. Instead, I held my breath and tried not to move. Talk about awkward. About a year ago, Janice talked about how she'd decorate the church for a wedding, but that was for the wedding that never happened, with Reid. The Camps weren't overzealous with religion, but a wedding tradition had formed. The last three generations had been married in the same church. I'd heard it before, as if I was also expected to get married someday in that very church. As an only child, if Shelby didn't keep the tradition going, then it'd fade away.

"We were thinking Nassawango, at the golf club." Shelby squeezed her eyes shut. Janice would still be upset, but at least Shelby could spare herself the look on her mother's face. "But we're still just getting ideas. Nothing's set in stone yet."

"Are you sure about this, Shel? I mean, you'd be breaking tradition," Janice said in a controlled voice, though her cheeks were flushed and eyes teary.

"Yes, it's what we both want," Shelby said as she opened her eyes and blinked.

"It would be a beautiful location. You'd be close to the river and could probably get a couple of pictures outside if it's not too cold," I added.

Janice was like a mother to me in so many ways. I didn't like to see her hurt.

"Exactly, and with the large windows, it'd feel more like we were outside. If Danny's house were bigger, we'd do it there," Shelby said. Her eyes danced like they did when she was excited.

"I bet you would." I held my hand over my mouth. No one needed sarcasm right now.

Shelby rolled her eyes at me, but she wasn't really angry.

"Okay then. You'll have to tell your father," Janice said. Shelby's father usually didn't put up much resistance, so problem solved.

"Thank you for understanding." Shelby reached out for her mother's hand.

Janice, with tears edging her lashes, looked at Shelby and squeezed her hand and smiled. "Are you ever warm?"

Shelby blushed. "No, my hands are usually cold."

"You should consider getting your blood checked. You might be anemic," Janice said. She looked worried again. "At the very least, you could be iron deficient."

"I don't think that's it. I'm okay. Just cold natured." Shelby's lips turned up in a wry smile. Her teeth gleamed like they'd recently been whitened.

Janice looked from Shelby to me. "So are we straight for today?"

"As far as I know," Shelby said.

"You've got to take these home with you. I thought you'd like them." Janice put the muffins into plastic baggies.

"Maybe Libby would like some too? Danny isn't a fan of blueberries, and I can only eat so many," Shelby said with her hand on her tiny stomach.

"I'll take a few. That'd be great."

Janice handed me a bag of muffins. I normally avoided sugar, but no doubt those muffins would disappear before breakfast tomorrow.

I walked outside with Shelby. At almost five in the evening, the dark sky glimmered with stars. I zipped my parka. Since Shelby had been with Danny, we hadn't hung out like we used to. I wondered if Danny approved of me. He seemed nice enough to my face, but was he the cause of my stagnating friendship with Shelby?

"So what are you doing tonight?" Maybe she'd want to have an early dinner.

"I've got to help Danny with his book tonight. He's nearly ready to publish it, and I'm helping him refine a couple passages."

So that was a no-go.

"Well, have fun with that."

She'd brushed me off...again. I wouldn't push it. Charity wasn't the kind of relationship I wanted with my best friend. I'd rather spend time alone in my town house. "How's Liam doing?" I'd only seen him once, but I couldn't get his face or his woodsy scent out of my head.

"He's fine. He's planning on building a log cabin near Danny's. The plans have been approved, so maybe he'll soon have a new house."

I'd hoped he'd ask for my phone number, but that hadn't happened. If Shelby was a better friend, she'd set us up. "Good for him."

"It feels like forever since I've seen you. Is there anything new I should know?"

So she was going to play it like this? Like my full schedule kept us from hanging out? Mouth diarrhea be damned! "Are you eating, Shelby? Because you've lost a lot of weight." At this point, what did it matter?

She was super skinny. Maybe she had an eating disorder?

"Of course I'm eating!"

"Can I see you eat a muffin then?" *Liar*... She usually carried at least fifteen more pounds than she does now.

"If it'll somehow prove to you that I'm okay, then I'll eat it." She squinted a look I'd never seen from her before, but I refused to back down.

I gestured to the bag of muffins she carried.

She opened the bag, and a nauseated expression crossed her face. She took a small bite, and then another until the muffin was gone. Would she throw up? Her skin looked greenish and clammy.

"Are you okay?"

"I'm fine," she said, but her eyes were tearing. "Are we still on for Thursday morning?"

She wasn't well. Maybe she really was pregnant, in which case I'd consider forgiving her for blowing me off.

"Yes. Thursday morning."

She gave me a hug, cool and emotionless, before she slid into her car. Were we even still friends?

***

A midweek slump hit as I toyed with new fabric swatches from the latest Ethan Allen collection. Light radiated through the open office space, which helped me to see the true color of the fabrics. I liked to compare fabric colors against paint samples. It made my job easier when I presorted them for my clients. This year's collection was understated but classic with navy variants paired with derby-brown accents. My desk sat out with the other desks. The only person who had any privacy was my boss, Mrs. Lillian Spencer. I liked being out where the action took place, but it made it impossible to check my phone or search the Internet for new designs without looking like a slacker.

"Hi, Libby, how are you doing today?" Christian asked. He stood with his arms crossed over a white button-down shirt, one jean-clad leg crossed over the other. He was clean cut with short blond hair and gorgeous blue eyes. Even with his good-looking face and perfectly sculpted body, he wasn't my type. He had a bad-boy rating of one on a one-to-ten scale. To top it off, we looked like siblings. Christian was my boss's son and was a successful restaurateur. Lillian had been trying to get us together for ages, but I didn't want to go there. If things turned sour, then it would affect my job. Plus, kissing him would be too much like kissing myself—far too weird.

"I'm good. How about you?" I wanted to be nice, but at the same time, not too nice.

He smiled a toothy grin that displayed his pristine white veneers. He'd be a good distraction from Liam, true, but other men could serve that purpose.

"Things are going well. We've expanded our selections at the restaurant, and I've finally got a few signature dishes on the dinner menu." His eyes lit up when he talked about the restaurant, but still no sparks.

We talked for a few minutes, and then he left for his restaurant. He always hesitated when he said good-bye, as if he wanted to say more. He stopped by sometimes on his way to work to see his mother, but his visits were usually around lunchtime, when he'd bring the office lunch. The food from his restaurant was five-star quality but affordable. I loved the citrus chicken over cranberry rice. Savory and sweet, it was something I couldn't get anywhere else.

Later in the morning, I worked on a room layout for one of the part-timers. She had a good eye for style and how things should be placed, but she was color blind. To avoid design disasters, I usually reviewed her designs before anything was ordered. We didn't need another clown-house situation. My eyes began to cross from the near constant strain on the computer screen, when my cell phone rang. *Didn't I put it on vibrate?* Lillian's door was shut, not that she'd say much about a personal call, but still... A man I'd gone on one date with, months ago, called. It was unexpected but could be the diversion I needed to get out of my *lonely and bored* funk. He asked me to his house for dinner. I couldn't turn down Sam "the cop" Thompson. His actual physical attributes were rather foggy, but from what I could remember, he was handsome, about six feet tall, with buzzed brown hair. We didn't click on our only date, but maybe this time would be better. Sam said he'd pick me up from my house since I didn't know where he lived. I usually liked to have my own car around for quick getaways, but if I wasn't safe with a cop, then I wouldn't be safe anywhere.

I took a quick shower after work. Not that I was sweaty, but I wanted to smell fresh. I wasn't sure what to wear for a night in, but opted for a semiformal cream-colored dress with a lace overlay.

It wasn't too dressy but still looked hot. I pulled my hair up into a French twist and fixed my makeup.

When his car pulled up to the curb, I turned off the inside lamps but kept on the lights in the foyer and front stoop. I watched as he climbed out of his patrol car. *So he didn't have a normal car too?* He strutted up the sidewalk like a rooster, but I'd forgive him this time. As he walked closer to the door, I noted he'd muscled up since I'd last seen him. Even his neck was more developed, like on a pit bull.

I opened the door to let him inside. His eyes raked me from my head to my knee-high boots.

"You look great, Lib." He seemed too comfortable with me, and I wasn't sure what to make of the unearned familiarity. Maybe that was why I'd cut him off after one date?

"You look good too, Sam. Have you been working out?" He looked like he'd probably taken steroids.

"It's that obvious?" He spread his arms out and turned in a circle. He wore a navy Henley shirt and dark jeans. The shirt fit tight across his chest.

"Wow." I wasn't impressed, but I didn't want to belittle him either. Big muscles were fine and all, but not really my thing.

"Are you ready?"

"Yes."

Sam was attractive in a meathead kind of way. I didn't want a relationship with this guy, but brief companionship would be nice. I ignored the bad vibe that skittered down my spine, and followed him with my purse in hand to his patrol car. I could only imagine the germs that festered inside his jailhouse on wheels. He didn't open the door for me, and I had to move empty wrappers from the seat before I sat down. After a brief drive to farm country, he pointed out his house, an unimpressive ranch-style surrounded by empty corn and soybean fields. Pig manure radiated from a field nearby…the worst of all manure fragrances.

He opened the car door and was halfway to the house, while I hesitantly opened my door. The heels of my boots sank into the muddy driveway. I tried to keep my weight on my toes to prevent my heels from sinking in any deeper. I followed Sam to the porch. The house was kind of cute but needed minor landscaping and maybe a fresh coat of paint on the porch and front door. The screen door hung by its hinges, but the storm door behind it was in good condition. I should've worn something less likely to stain, hindsight being what it was.

This would be my last date with Sam.

Once inside, he took my wrap and purse. I wondered if maybe there was some hope for a nice evening after all. He had good manners, at the very least.

"Have a seat." His hand rested on my lower back as he directed me to the kitchen table. His touch sent shivers up my spine, the kind that were reminiscent of an inappropriate uncle. *Not good.*

The table was set for two. Though not fancy, it looked like he'd tried. The table itself was either a hand-me-down or came with the house. He'd at least made an attempt at cooking. He kept the prepared food in the oven but insisted on starting the evening with a cocktail. He motioned for me to take a seat at the enamel table, and he presented me with a mixture of cranberry juice, pineapple juice, and vodka. I sipped the beverage to appease him. It was bitter, but I forced it down. No doubt he'd used cheap liquor.

He looked so eager to please me. His mouth curled into a grin at my emptied glass.

"How did you like it?"

My focus blurred like it sometimes did when I hadn't eaten. The liquor had been too strong. I tried to speak, but my words slurred. Something was wrong. "Sammmm," I garbled. The expression on his face changed. His eyes held a darkness I couldn't understand. I tried to stand up, but my legs were Jell-O. I crashed to the floor. "Please…" I managed to whisper.

Sam knelt by my side as I lay on the floor, unable to stand. He caressed my cheek. "You're so pretty, Libby."

I tried to move from his touch, but it was useless.

"Girls like you need to be taught a lesson."

What the hell? He's delusional…

He pulled me into his massive arms. My legs hit against the dark-paneled doorway as he carried me down the short hall. I couldn't resist, my body sagging in his arms.

I peed as he carried me. It was the only act of defiance I could muster. Maybe it'd dissuade him from further acts?

"That's disgusting! You little bitch!" His grip only tightened, and when we entered what seemed to be a bedroom, he dropped me on the bed without any sympathy. The bed was messy, and knots of balled-up sheets poked at my back. He grabbed my wrists and handcuffed them to the frame of the metal bed. There was no use in resisting, as I guessed he drugged me. I forced my eyes shut to lessen the vertigo that had me spinning in place. Once the door slammed closed, I looked around the room. The walls seemed to ripple but were plain, no phone, nothing for me to free myself with. No one would hear my screams here—there were no close neighbors. I would probably die here…

My breathing quickened. I wasn't ready to die! The facts made it unlikely that I'd ever leave this place alive. He was a police officer. He would know how to dispose of me without getting caught. Tears burned my cheeks. My heart raced like my chest would explode. From panic came exhaustion. The drug that pumped through my veins along with the liquor had won. I couldn't keep my eyes open and somehow resigned myself to the fact that I'd die here, maybe even tonight. I dreaded the moment Sam would return.

***

Liam

Spread across Danny's living room floor were hardwood and bamboo flooring samples from Lumber Liquidators. I fit together mismatching samples from the easy-click collection. There was something satisfying in how samples that seemed to be different in every way still fit together, as if that'd been the intention all along. Danny was yet to complain about looking at cabinet and flooring samples with me, and that was after hours of product comparison and indecision. He humored my house-building distraction with the expected compassion of a brother who knew I needed something to get reality off of my mind. We'd spent at least two hours on flooring samples alone weighing the pros and cons of style, durability, and brand, but still anything shared deeper wasn't yet welcomed…new wounds still too raw. Our relationship was strained, not because of lacking care but from decades of separation. It might have been easier had I not recently lost my wife, but that fate wasn't something that could've been anticipated.

I'd soon have roots here on a lot adjacent to Danny's house. He'd been generous enough to sell me ten acres of his property. He wanted to gift me the land, but it'd never really be mine without the exchange of money or my name on its plot. He'd bought as much land as he could in one area for privacy and hunting. Human neighbors wouldn't welcome us if they knew what we were, which meant barriers were a necessity. Not that the property itself boasted gates or walls, but the size of the property provided a natural separation from human dwellings. I'd never owned property, even though I lived entire life spans in a few different places. I couldn't give Ciara a real home, not like she deserved. I'd always been too afraid to settle down, having worried that it would raise suspicion if we stayed in one place too long. Danny had done his homework, and he kept properties in circulation for when he needed to get away for a while. Why hadn't I thought of that?

Both Danny and Shelby welcomed me into their home, but they needed time to themselves. Besides, I wanted my own space too. The house plan I settled on was by the same designer as Danny's house, only it was almost a thousand square-feet larger. After having lived in meager huts and other "cozy" spaces with Ciara, this house would make up for all that I'd neglected for far too long. Ireland had been home, but now I didn't have long-term goals. I'd have a house and would worry about my next step when it presented itself.

For the past decade I'd worked as a freelance business consultant, mostly computer work and phone consultations. Not that I needed that much money to live, but the paychecks were a perk. The one thing that work brought was peace. I'd given it up during my travels to locate Danny, but before that I consulted for start-up businesses to full-blown corporations, and for some reason my clients' stresses made my own worries abate. Having cash on hand also made the building process seamless. I'd soon depart with a hefty chunk of money for the large intact cypress logs that would encase the house structure. Without Ciara around to occupy my mind, purpose and diversion gave me solace. She had to be better off wherever she was now though…right? I'd always thought Ciara would be my only wife and love, but now I wasn't sure. The love that I'd felt for her paled to more emergent emotions I'd been forced to face. Not that I didn't love her, but it'd been difficult living with someone who resented me. Deep down, she never let me off the hook for destroying her soul. Not that I could blame her for that.

With the first taste of Libby's blood, everything changed. I didn't need to taste her to know something was different about her, but how could I resist? It wasn't her gorgeous face, not even her rounded warm body, but her essence called to me. Rational thought screamed to keep my distance from her. A weak human was a fruitless pursuit. But I had to know for sure she was different. Her blood awoke something I tried to hide, but what did it all mean? If I changed her—like I had Ciara—she'd hate me. I prayed that Ciara had made it to another realm, not that prayers from a vampire had any pull. Libby would eventually hate me too, once she knew what I really was. Not that I'd seen her since that first time.

Since Ciara's death, my tracking abilities amplified, as if she'd transferred them to me. Darker elements also came with my heightened abilities. Sometimes I didn't feel alone in the forest. An eeriness had descended, and I felt like spirits passed through me at unpredictable times. Maybe I was going crazy?

"So what were you thinking? Maple or pine?" Danny asked as he held a sample in each hand.

I blinked and refocused my attention on him. "I don't know. I was thinking something exotic, like Brazilian pecan." I plucked the multitonal sample from the pile. The color pattern in the exotic sample was unexpected…like me. The wood ranged from a pale maple to a deep mahogany and was precisely what I wanted. From here on out, I was going to get what I wanted—within reason, of course.

"It sounds like you have that one figured out then. What about the kitchen cabinets? Are you going to go with a natural wood or painted?" Danny's expression was serious for something so trivial.

"I don't know. Maybe blood-red cabinets." It wasn't like I was going to really use them. The only food I consumed was out of a vein. A Sub-Zero refrigerator would be a better investment. Bagged blood tasted better when the temperature was kept at a stable six degrees Celsius.

"So no house-warming party? I was going to get you a toaster oven." Danny nudged my shoulder and laughed.

"Sorry, no house-warming party. The finger foods would be a nightmare."

"Did you know that Libby is an interior designer? You could hire her to coordinate your designs. Shelby says that she's really good." Danny raised his brow.

I wasn't stupid. What was he thinking? My attempts to hide my attraction to her hadn't been as impenetrable as I'd thought, not that I hadn't noticed how Shelby treated me like a ticking time bomb. I'd seen a few human and vampire romances before, and they were normal in some ways, but it was such a gamble. Sexually, every nerve in my body wanted Libby, but if she found out what I was, then what? I couldn't tell her my secret—she'd be frightened, or worse, she might want me to change her.

Shelby's transition had gone better than expected. It was like she was made to be a vampire, though she was still so new to it all. This lifestyle had a required taste, and Libby might not be up for any part of it. *But what if she didn't find out…*

"I don't know if that would be a good idea." Denial that I had any attraction to Libby would be the easiest to feign, but it'd be unbelievable.

"Why not? You have control of yourself, and she could make the design process a lot easier." Danny sounded like her biggest fan, though I doubted he really cared for her.

"There's something about her. I don't know how much control I have over myself. Her scent…the taste of her blood hasn't left my mind. That's not normal." I pushed my hands through my hair, trying to escape her pull. Ripples of memory raced back to when I'd held her. She'd been weak, subdued. I could've been a real threat to her, but I'd held her like she was a precious gift.

Danny's voice softened. Instead of the demanding tone he'd first had, it was more pleading. He put his hand on my shoulder. "Maybe you should give in. It might be what you need. God knows that Shelby saved me from monotony."

"Yes, but how fair would it be to Libby? She doesn't know what I am, what we all are. If I were in her shoes, I'd run the other way and never look back." I couldn't believe that anyone would choose this life—despite the immortality perk, it was unnatural.

"I don't think you're being fair to yourself. You don't have any way of knowing how she'll react if you don't give her a chance." Danny's hand dropped from my shoulder. "Liam, I didn't think I'd ever see you again, and now that we have each other, I want you to be happy too."

"I want to be happy, but I already ruined Ciara's life. I think I'm out of chances for a happily ever after."

"I don't think it works that way. Please consider it, and if things don't work out between the two of you on a professional level, then you can end your agreement."

"I'll think about it." I placed the samples back in the box they'd come in and would return them to the contractor. The flooring would be the Brazilian pecan, but the cabinets were still up in the air, as were all the other furnishings. Maybe an interior designer would be the best bet, though I didn't know if I'd subject Libby to that job just yet.

The doorbell rang, and all thoughts of Libby fell away. Danny had disappeared in his office, and I went to the door. A smiling FedEx delivery man stood there with what I presumed was the laptop I'd ordered.

"Do you play basketball?" The delivery man asked as he took in my height. His brown eyes were wide and doe-like.

I smiled. He wasn't the first to ask that. "No, never have."

"Too bad… How tall are you anyway?" He met my eyes.

I took the electronic signature pad from his hands and signed it. "I'm six foot five."

"Every bit of it," he said with a courteous nod. He handed me the carrying handle of the box. "See you around."

"Thank you," I said as he walked back toward his truck.

I sliced through the shipping tape and slid out the new Dell Precision M3800 Mobile Workstation. The capabilities of this laptop were extensive, and considering my line of work, I needed something that could better handle what I threw at it. I'd used Danny's computer to reestablish some of my old connections, but it'd lacked the programs I needed to effectively do my job. Now I could get to work.

I'd set up a temporary work area in Danny's guest room, which I also slept in. Soon I'd have a proper office in my own house. I settled my laptop on the queen-sized bed. If I worked most of the evening, I wouldn't have to think about interior design, Shelby's insistence that I stay away from her friend, or even Danny pushing for me to hire Libby. When at work, my mind rebooted itself. A few keystrokes later, I had my first new client.

***

Liam, Saint Patrick's Day, Thursday, 2016

By the next afternoon, my legs warmed to the weight and battery of the new Dell laptop. I would be working exclusively with Domino Hives starting sometime next week. Domino was a small bee farm that produced its own honey, and the owners needed help to get their products on local shelves. Their main operation ran out of their own store and local farmers' markets. It should be an easy gig and would help me to ease back into business society and get my name out there again. Today was Saint Patrick's Day, which didn't mean much here and was only marked by humans drinking mass quantities of green beer. St. Paddy's would mean something more at home in Ireland. Its excitement would filter through the air. Though I'd long suspected that much of the celebration had to do with the banishment of my kind... Irish locals had no idea of the serpents that still slithered underfoot, or mingled with the humans, as it were.

The front door slammed, and seconds later Shelby stood at the end of my bed, panting. Her hair was windblown, and she wore an unsettled expression. She tried to catch her breath. Even though she didn't need oxygen to live, it was a hard reaction to break.

"I can't find Libby. She was supposed to meet me this morning, but she wasn't at home." Shelby paused and took a deep breath. "She won't answer her phone, and I drove by her office. She's not there either."

Shelby's panic melted into my chest, but I tried to hold a rational front. I moved the laptop aside and met Shelby where she stood. I eased her down until she was sitting on the edge of my bed.

"What time were you supposed to meet her?"

"Nine. She knew I'd be coming over. She didn't have to go into work until noon." Shelby's eyes were wet with tears.

I glanced over at my bedside table. The clock read 10:20. "Could she have forgotten about your plans?" Fear constricted my throat.

"No way. Even if she did somehow forget, she'd answer her phone. It must still be on, because it didn't take me directly to her voice mail. Something has happened to her." She picked at her fingernails.

I could track now—I'd find her. Danny was out hunting, but I couldn't take Shelby with me. She was too green for this ordeal, though leaving her alone wasn't ideal.

The hardwood floors creaked as I paced. Libby had her shortcomings. From what little I knew of her, she seemed reckless and unconcerned about her own safety. I sensed an accident or unexpected adventure wasn't the culprit. Was she with someone she trusted? I concentrated on Libby—the taste of her blood, the smell of her skin, the small inhalation sounds she made as she breathed. My body called itself into action as if I was being pulled by an external force.

"Stay here, Shelby. As soon as I find her, you'll be the first to know. If Danny comes back before I return, please tell him to stay with you. I don't want to leave you alone, but it has to be like this. I'll find your friend." I grabbed my wool coat and headed outdoors. Instead of turning to the forest like I did so many times before, I followed the road. I could've taken Shelby's car, but I worried that the hum of the car's engine would alter my senses. Ciara used to say she tracked by scent alone. The scent of Libby was there in memory, but something else was stronger. Was I imagining it?

I drummed up every memory of Libby I could remember: her fine, bouncy blond hair, her placid blue eyes, her nearly transparent skin, her blood. Once in the city limits, recognition flared. I found her town house, though nothing called to me from within the structure. Without her inside, the town house was like a soulless body. Her white Mazda SUV was parked in the front parking space. The town house looked like the others around it, except for small details that could've only been contrived by Libby. The flower boxes, which were flowerless for the time being, were painted hot pink. The doormat was feminine and boasted wineglasses. The open curtains revealed a sliver of a zebra-patterned sofa. As I stood on the wineglass doormat, urgency flooded my limbs.

I couldn't help but run. I slowed the pace, but my legs burned as I limited myself, as if my body was begging to go faster. I wound up in the country. Manure-covered fields peppered the landscape—all too dirty for Libby. A small plain-looking house sat on the horizon, though its true shabbiness stood out the closer I ran. Something about the dingy white rancher sparked my interest. I had to check it out. The scene was wrong. The patrol car in the muddy driveway questioned my need to investigate the house, but with a grimace I forced myself to look inside. I cleared dusty mud from a window and saw a man passed out in a recliner. His muscles bulged, but empty beer bottles surrounded his chair on the floor. The side window was even dirtier, but as I peeked through a space in the askew mini blinds, I caught movement on what looked like a bed. I almost lost my footing when the horizontal figure turned its head. Libby's delicate face pointed in my direction, though her eyes remained closed. She was restrained, her wrists secured above her head. I rushed to the front entrance and banged on the door. The porch's floorboards shifted as the large man moved from inside. He opened the door and squinted as he looked me up and down. He looked smug, clearly taunting me. It only fueled the fire in my veins.

"Can I help you?" asked the man rhetorically. His body was massive, but I had several inches on him. He was a fool to think he had the upper hand.

"I'm here for Libby Anderson," I said as I pushed past him. In my peripheral vision, his arm winded back to hit me, but I shoved back his attack before it could land. The motion caused him to spin off kilter. *Was he serious?*

"Son of a bitch!" He held his side. "Get out of my house! I'll arrest you!"

He'd pay for what he'd done. I kicked his legs until I heard both femurs snap as he crumpled to the hardwood floor. He didn't stand a chance. "If you ever come near her again, or touch a hair on any woman's head, I'll be back to finish you. You can count on it!" I stared at him until he met my eyes. Understanding and belief reflected in his pained gaze. Had I the foresight, I'd tattoo "abuser" on his forehead.

He moaned and sobbed. "You're a monster!" he screamed as he scooted on his elbows. He was right—not that I cared. If I found out that he'd done anything to Libby, he'd be dead. I'd have no choice. As it stood, pressing charges on him would've been pointless. He was a part of the judicial system, though he was tainted and likely mentally disturbed.

I found Libby with her arms handcuffed on the metal bed frame. She looked like an injured bird. Small, frail, and shaking. Her eyes were closed, as if that would protect her from what was to come.

"Libby." I tried to unhook the handcuffs but couldn't risk hurting her. She just trembled. I found the key on the dresser, well out of her reach. Unlocking the first cuff, I steadied her arm down by her side while supporting the other arm. Libby whimpered at the movement. I dropped the cuffs to the floor. She turned to the wall, eyes still closed. A chemical tang wafted off her skin. She'd been drugged. Other human scents drifted up too—sweat, urine, and adrenaline. I pushed under her body and lifted her from the stained and wrinkled bedding. Her head rested against my chest, and she sighed. The only way out was through the living room and past the attacker. The man lay moaning, prone on the floor. His belly rose with his respirations, but nothing else moved. Killing him wasn't my intention, but it wouldn't have been a great loss either. I looped Libby's purse around my neck and pushed through the storm door. The air was chilly but not as halting as it'd been days before.

I took a deep cleansing breath. Manure smelled better than that house had. Libby was safer now, but she'd need an examination at the very least. She couldn't walk…at least not yet. Danny's place would be too far on foot, but Libby's town house wasn't that far away, and she'd be in familiar surroundings there. Besides, she looked the worse for wear. My go-to story if anyone asked would be that she was sick. I ran when I could and kept her cradled against my chest. She was so warm. I'd forgotten just how warm humans were. Her body trembled, but a drug haze wearing off would have that effect. Twenty minutes later we were on the stoop of her town house. The key was in her purse. I opened the door to hot-pink walls.

I couldn't put her in bed like this, not with the filth from the rancher. Instead I stretched out the blanket from the back of the sofa and laid her on it. Once lucid, she could bathe and get into her bed.

I called Shelby's cell phone number. It was programmed into Libby's phone. When Shelby answered, she sounded tense but calmed as I spoke. I summarized the events and told her I would take care of Libby until she roused. Shelby wanted to come over, but not yet. She'd stay with Danny until I could sort this out. Libby was frail and would be my responsibility until she could tell me otherwise.

Chapter 2

Reprieve

Libby

I raised my arms and stretched out, amazed I could move without restriction. Was I dreaming or dead? Was sleep even possible in death, because I was groggy, not at all refreshed like the afterlife should have made me. Opening my eyes would mean reality, which I could do without for now. I couldn't begin to fathom what Sam had planned for me next...

I took a deep breath and couldn't understand where the scent of manure and old-house funk had gone. Curiosity won out as I peeped out through lowered lashes. I balled my fists to ready my defenses but realized I was home and still seemingly in one piece. My fingers traced the crocheted blanket that rested under my body. It was lime green and felt furry, like a stuffed animal. I smelled terrible, like a goats' pen. I wasn't a farm girl, but I knew animal scents from living on the Eastern Shore of Maryland my entire life. Just how had I gotten here? Gone was the visceral fear that plagued me before. Since I was home, I had to be safe now... *Right?* I looked over the back of the sofa. The sound of my pulse pounded in my ears. I saw no one. Was I alone?

"How are you feeling?" A warm masculine voice asked. The unexpected presence startled me. I would've jumped if I wasn't so tender.

I turned toward the voice and saw Liam sitting in a chair near the sofa. He hadn't made a sound. I lay down on my back, giving into the soreness. My arms and ribs hurt to move, and my breathing pressed down on my sternum. "What happened?" I asked, but I really wanted to know how I'd come out of there alive. I still wore the evidence of what'd happened, as if the memory alone could've ever been forgotten. My obsession watched my every move. His gaze was unreadable but comforted me nonetheless.

"You were supposed to meet Shelby today, and when she couldn't find you, she got worried." Liam seemed calm, but a storm brewed in his eyes. Was he trying to protect me from all that had happened by leaving out the gory details?

"How did you find me? I'm grateful that you did, but it should have been next to impossible." I was in the country, and no one but Sam knew where I was. On top of that, Sam was a police officer. How on earth would anyone suspect him of keeping a hostage? It wasn't like I had a relationship with Sam. How did Liam piece it all together?

A troubled expression crossed Liam's face. "If I told you, there'd be no way you'd believe me." His sandy-brown hair stuck out in different directions, but despite that, he looked angelic. His magnificence was unusual. He was pale, but that only heightened the contrast of his features. Liam and Danny shared so many physical traits, but Liam was more polished, a gentleman.

"Try me." I could take anything now that I'd lived to tell.

"Let's just call it intuition." He looked playful but guarded. He didn't seem to be in the mood to elaborate.

"Intuition?" I let it hang in the air. "I wouldn't be mad if you were following me." I'd follow him if it would be worthwhile, but I didn't think something that childish could win him over.

He looked annoyed. "I wasn't following you. I'm not a stalker, Libby." His voice was flat.

Had I offended him?

"Sorry. I didn't mean to make you angry. I just don't understand." I tried to meet his gaze, but he looked away. "I was so convinced that I was going to die, and when I woke up here…I wondered how I survived."

"I don't think he would've killed you. From what I could guess, he was punishing you. I'm so sorry you had to experience this."

I tried not to cry, but my breath caught, and I couldn't help it. I wasn't sure how punishment was any better than death, but I was glad to be alive. I didn't know if I could trust anyone enough to date again as it stood. Tears ran down my cheeks, and I wiped at them until my sleeve was wet. Liam came over and sat by my legs. I pushed myself into a semi-sitting position. He'd grabbed a handful of tissues from the coffee table and dabbed at my face. This only made me cry harder. He opened his arms, and I nestled into him. His chest was solid and made me feel minuscule in comparison.

"Are you going to tell me why you'd go out with such a lowlife?"

I closed my eyes and focused on Liam's breath in my hair.
"I had to get you out of my head. I needed a distraction."

His body stiffened, but he didn't let go.

"Are you saying that you went out with him in an attempt to forget about me? I hadn't meant to lead you on, Libby. I'm sorry if I did."

Body-shaking quakes rippled through me, and crying turned into sobs. I moved away from him but was so sore that I remained on the sofa. "You can leave then..." Though every cell of my body wanted him near. I'd always choose loneliness over pity.

"I don't want to leave you, and it's not because I think you need someone around." He paused and cleared his throat. His Irish accent was thicker than I'd ever heard him speak. "I feel something for you, an attraction, but I'm also recently widowed." He pulled me back into his arms.

Wasn't he too young to be a widow? "What?" Suddenly my situation seemed to pale next to his. How could I push myself on a man recovering from such a loss? Yet I couldn't deny my own feelings either.

"Yes. My wife passed away not long before Shelby's engagement."

"How did she die?" I didn't want to ask but had to know.

"It was an accident," he said without expansion, though his body was more unyielding than it had been.

"I'm sorry. I didn't know." What else was there to say to that?

"It's okay. We had a long marriage."

Did he get married when he was a teenager? "Just how long were you married?"

He cleared his throat again. "What I meant to say is that we were together for a long time, not that we were married that long. We grew up as friends." His words came out in a rush.

So was this why he seemed unavailable, or maybe I only wanted a man who couldn't reciprocate my affection? I was messed up when it came to relationships, but this was the most awkward scenario I'd ever been in. Still, I snuggled in his embrace, glad for the comfort.

He remained silent a few moments, but then the stiffness of his body eased. "I feel drawn to you, and I don't know if I can shake it off or not. I tried to avoid you and went out of my way to be out of the house when you came to visit Shelby, but I can't do it anymore. It's too draining." He paused and turned me so that I could see his hazel eyes as he spoke. "I know you just went through an ordeal, and if you don't want me, it's okay. But please tell me now, or I won't be able to get you out of my head. I know it's a lot to take in, and you still will have to get to know me more before you make any lasting decisions. I'd be lying if I told you that I'm your best option. Make no mistake—I'm not. You could do better. You'd just have to be more cautious with screening your suitors."

Was this a warning or an invitation? Since day one I would've taken him, no matter how equally screwed up he was. I'd used him as a scale ever since he came into my life, and no one else could ever measure up. I could warn him about my own faults, but he already knew I wasn't perfect.

"You know what I want," I said in a tone so low that I wasn't sure if he'd heard me.

"I was afraid you'd say that." His arms wrapped around me in a way that made me feel like I was his possession. Like he would live and die for me, and that made me wonder what he'd done to Sam, not that I wanted anything but revenge for him.

"Will Sam bother me again?"

"No, and if he does, it will be the end of him."

There was no doubting his sincerity. At least I was safe for now. Being here with Liam was what I wanted. We were both damaged, and I could live with that…

"Can I help you to change?" Liam asked, his eyes raking over my stained dress.

This was his polite way of saying that I smelled like a barn. After Sam drugged me, he had picked me up to carry me to the bedroom, and I'd peed all over him. Though it had seemed like a loss of bladder control brought on by whatever drug he'd given me, it wasn't accidental. Maybe my plan had worked, since he hadn't touched me after he'd cuffed me to the bed. I'd almost grown used to the smell after all that had happened, but Liam was right. I needed to freshen up.

"I need a shower." Changing my clothes wouldn't help since the dirt and urine were on my skin. A PTA, or pits, tits, and ass, sink bath wouldn't even come close to quenching the stench. I sniffed at a lock of hair…I'd have to rinse and repeat.

"I'm here if you need help," Liam offered.

He wasn't being a pervert—he sounded sincere. He was different from the other men I'd been attracted to. He didn't force himself on me, though my current aroma was enough to keep stray dogs at length. I pushed off the sofa and winced. A sore throbbing radiated from my pelvis and centered on my hip. I started to fall back onto the sofa, but Liam's large hands braced me. I was able to displace the pressure that'd caused the pain.

"Thank you." I held his forearms for support.

"You need help." He wasn't asking. He scooped me up into his arms.

"Whoa!" I held on to his shoulders with a death grip. I couldn't have been peeled off him at this point.

"Your bathroom is which way?" He looked side to side.

I pointed toward the stairs. Even though I had a bathroom on the main level, all of my stuff was in the one upstairs. He scaled the staircase effortlessly. I always left the bathroom door open, and he gently sat me down on the toilet, of all places… I was a queen on her throne. I usually took showers, but that would be impossible. The only other option would be a bath. How would I get out of the bathtub though? Liam stood there, his tall form blocking the dim evening light that glowed through the skylight. He flicked the vanity lights on. Once the room was illuminated, it was obvious this was going to be a tricky situation.

"I don't mean to point this out to you, but you're going to need me."

My stomach knotted at the thought of him helping me bathe. There was nothing sexy about being incapacitated.

"Would you rather I call Shelby, or maybe your mother?"

No, and no!

He seemed to anticipate my apprehension, but those options were even worse than having his assistance. My mom lived a good hour away, so that wasn't a viable option, and I didn't want to bother Shelby. Not that I wanted either of them with me when I was naked...that'd be all kinds of weird and wrong. I took a deep breath. I'd undressed in front of men before. Why was this any different? The answer presented itself—because I really felt something for him. He wasn't a random guy. He was special.

Liam started the water in the bathtub. I watched as he added bubbles, which would screen me once I was submerged. I pulled the dress over my head and dropped it right into the trash can. It was ruined now. I sat on the toilet in my bra, ripped-up leggings, and panties. Once the water reached a deep enough level for bathing, it was time to shed the rest of my clothes.

"I won't look." Liam turned his head to the side and pulled me to my feet.

He pulled down my leggings as I held on to the wall. He squatted down to free my feet one by one from the garment. My injured hip made it more difficult, but Liam managed to remove the leggings with minimal assistance.

Liam's eyes darted to my injured hip as if he couldn't fight the curiosity of seeing its severity. The bruise was a deep shade of purple. I watched as he drew his face closer to the bruise. I froze in place, not wanting to break his trance. His lips traced over my hip as he kissed along the injury. My breath caught in my throat.

"This will help you heal quicker," he said as if he was serious. That was the smoothest excuse I'd ever heard. How could a kiss accelerate healing?

Liam braced me by the rib cage with his head to the side so that I was as shielded from him as possible. I unhooked my bra and pushed down my panties. He guided me into the bathtub, all while still looking away. The water was hot and warmed my skin on contact. I laid back to soak, and moaned.

"Are you okay?" His gaze locked on me, though the bubbles covered me like I was under a fluffy comforter.

"Umhmmm." I closed my eyes.

"While you're soaking, I think I'll straighten up downstairs. I'd better get that green blanket into the wash."

I nodded but focused on the soothing water that helped to relax my bunched-up muscles. I dipped my head back and let my hair drift out in the water. It also needed to soak out the strange smells it'd absorbed. Finally, after a solid ten minutes of soaking, I was ready to scrub. I washed what I could of my skin and hair. I even tried to move my injured hip by bending my leg and holding a stretch, and for some reason it seemed less sore than it had earlier. The hot-water soak must have worked its magic. Maybe I could stand on it now, but pulling myself out of the water would still be a challenge. I pushed on the sides of the tub to move myself upward. Standing on my own wouldn't be graceful, but I could do it. There wasn't a handrail to hold on to, but there were ledges on the bathtub. So far, so good. When I was ready to stand, my feet slid. I tried again, only this time I pushed my upper body back farther and hoped that I'd have better control. This time I had it. I stood upright, and when my hip clicked into place, pain rushed down my leg. "Aaaah!" My vision blurred as my balance gave way. Instead of the bathtub's edge and floor bracing my fall...Liam caught me. I blinked away the blur and looked up into his eyes, and only then did I realize that I was completely naked in his clothed arms. My seal-slick skin shone in the vanity light. I scrambled to cover myself with my arms, as if that would make him forget what he'd already seen. Liam's hold didn't falter, and he was somehow able to pull a towel off the rack and wrap me in its shelter.

"I'm guessing that falling out of the bathtub wasn't your plan?" Liam grinned as he stood up with me in his arms.

I didn't care and let my dripping-wet hair lay against his chest. "No, falling wasn't the plan." I shivered as splats of water dropped off my head onto the floor.

"How about we get you dressed?"

I nodded. He carried me to my bedroom and set me on the bed. I held the towel close to bottle up any lingering warmth it still held. I directed him to the dresser that held my nightclothes, and he helped me into a silky night gown and matching robe. Getting my panties on would take submission, so I lay back and allowed Liam to guide them up and over my sore hip. He didn't even try to look and was a gentleman the entire process. Though it'd be nice if he'd at least try to sneak a peek…

Liam's eyes met mine. Something about his gaze transfixed me, and for a second I couldn't guess what he'd say. "Libby." His tone was clear but husky. Without waiting for me to answer, he kept talking. "Did he violate you in any way?"

So we had to go there. My heart sank for the pain he tried to hide. Maybe he thought he'd come too late? "No, no, nothing like that. He didn't actually touch much after tying me up. I'm not even sure what he meant to do. I was scared of what could've happened, but he never came back into the room, that I can remember anyway. I'm sure I smelled too bad to approach as it was."

My stomach growled loud enough to be heard rooms away. For once this was a welcomed noise—it took away from the other issues at hand. I didn't skip meals, but I hadn't eaten since the evening before, if that even counted.

Liam held his index finger over his lips like he was thinking. The heaviness had lifted from his gaze. "What would you like to eat?"

I pushed up on decorative bed pillows and held my hand over my stomach to try and quell the hollow sounds. "Anything from the refrigerator would be fine. I think I might have a turkey dinner in the freezer."

"You'll need your strength. I'm sure I'll find something downstairs."

I turned the television on to drown out the silence after he went downstairs. TLC had a show on alternative health and Reiki healing. Not that I believed a kiss could help an injured hip, but there were similarities to what Liam had done that were somewhat like the principles of Reiki.

About twenty minutes later, Liam returned carrying a tray of food. I scrambled for the remote to turn off the television. He couldn't have guessed the connection I'd made, but still… He sat beside me on the bed, his weight shifting my balance toward him. The tray he'd brought had more food on it than I could eat in an entire day. There were grapes, banana slices, strawberries, fruit dip, cheese and crackers, and a small crock of what smelled like French onion soup.

"You're hungry too, right?"

"No, I had something while you were in the bath." He wouldn't have had enough time for a proper meal. Maybe he had a snack?

I forced myself to pace as I ate. As hungry as I was, only so much food would fit. My fingers shook as I spooned up the first taste of soup. Part of it went down my chin and neck.

"Allow me," Liam said as he took the crock and spoon from my hands. Fighting him seemed so futile, so I let him feed me. He was patient and wiped my chin every time a wayward drop fell. I finished the soup and ate most of the fruit and a few of the crackers. My limbs grew heavier, as if I hadn't slept in days.

"You should rest."

"I have to use the bathroom first." It was as if the soup's liquid content had gone straight to my bladder.

"Okay, let me help you then."

I didn't protest this time. Of course I needed help, or I'd be worse off. I held his hands as he pulled me upright. "Thank you, Liam. I'm sure that taking care of me like this wasn't on your list of things to do."

"I don't mind being here for you like this. If it were other circumstances…it'd probably be nice to have this intimacy."

I smiled, wishing we'd been brought together by other means, but wondered if that would've happened on its own. Maybe not.

He helped me to the restroom and waited outside the door. I halfway sat on the counter as I brushed my teeth. I called for Liam, who carried me back to bed. I didn't think he was trying to be romantic by toting me around—no, he was just practical. Liam tucked me in, kissed my forehead, and stroked me from my cheek to jaw. His touch was simple but made me feel safe. Right now safety was something I needed. My nerves had been stripped raw, but I was coming around.

"Sleep well…you'll be good as new soon."

I closed my eyes, believing him. I couldn't repay how he made me feel, both treasured and protected. As long as he was near, I'd be okay.

***

Liam

The next morning, I watched through the foyer windows as Shelby stepped out of her car. It was obvious she wanted to be with Libby, which was why I'd called her at seven in the morning. Leaving even for a short while was hard, but I had no other options. Trace scents of dirt and Sam's blood lingered on my pants and shirt sleeves. The urge to hunt called to me more than any other force. After being alone with Libby for so many hours, I had to feed. What I'd eaten two days ago was already metabolized. Danny had once said how his appetite was heightened when he was around Shelby while she was still human, and now I knew what he meant. My mouth was dry as sand, and only one thing could break through the drought—blood.

"Thanks for coming," I said to Shelby as she stepped inside of the town house. She was beautiful, but the hollows of her eyes were almost plum. She must not have slept. It was unsaid, but resentment and suspicion still served to separate Shelby from me. She couldn't know how I cared for Libby. I'd have to give her more time. Of course, Shelby could understand the attraction that connected Libby to someone like me. Hurting Libby was something I couldn't fathom, especially after what she'd been through now. It was ironic how much Shelby distrusted me when she'd been in the same situation with Danny.

"Is she still asleep?" Shelby whispered.

"Yes, and she'll probably be out a few more hours. She was drained when she finally fell asleep last night."

"Drained?" Shelby asked, as if I'd made Libby my meal.

"Tired." I scowled before forcing my face to relax. "She'll also need help getting around. She's hurt her hip."

"I think I can manage that. Did she eat anything?" Shelby asked in a tone that suggested I'd forgotten the human requirement for nourishment.

"If you mean did I feed her anything, then the answer would be yes, of course I did." Shelby had to know that I'd take care of her friend like I'd promised...*like I wanted to do*, but she still struggled to see my competence.

Shelby's tight expression lessened. "Thanks for everything. God only knows what would've happened if you hadn't gotten to her when you did."

Was she starting to come around to the idea that I wasn't out to drain her friend like a draft of Guinness? "There's nothing to thank me for," I said as I let myself out.

"You can take the car," Shelby said from the front stoop.

Driving back home might have been the logical thing to do, but I needed to move. The more static I remained, the more I needed to move my body despite exhaustion. I walked until I met tree cover. The sun was already high on the horizon and taunted me as it leached what little energy I had left. On my way home I came across a possum, but I passed it by. It was undersized and wouldn't even begin to curb the desert in my throat that grew with every passing minute. For some reason my tracking wasn't at its prime. Tracking, like anything else, needed rest to be functional. My last and only option would be to drink bagged human blood. It was something that I didn't want to acquire a taste for, as I worried that it'd make me more disposed to crave human blood.

When Ciara and I lived in Ireland, we sometimes dined on fresh human blood. Most of the time we fed on drunks since their memories would've been compromised to begin with, but the alcohol came through into the blood, making it taste stale and bitter. Though back in those days with Ciara, we took advantage of what we could get without drawing attention to ourselves. There weren't bagged-blood services at that time, nor even now in Ireland.

"Liam," Danny called as I walked through the living room.

Danny emerged from his office wearing nearly identical purple eye discolorations that Shelby bore. He wouldn't have let Shelby stay up all night by herself.

"How's Libby doing?"

I blinked a few times to adjust to the indoor lighting. "She's well. Sore, but she'll be fine." Sexy as hell even after being mistreated and bruised... When I held her slick, naked body I thought that my every wish had finally come true. I wasn't under any delusions and was well aware that she was high maintenance, appearance obsessed, and influenced by celebrities. Shelby loved Libby and talked about her a lot, in an attempt, I think, to discourage any attraction Shelby thought I might have for her friend. Little did Libby know that she was stunning without makeup, styled hair, or designer labels. Deep down it all had to be about insecurity and the need for acceptance. I'd like to help her with that, if she could accept me for what I was...

"Have you eaten yet?"

I shook my head.

Danny's hand rested on my shoulder as he guided me down the flight of stairs to the basement.

There was no denying my hunger. God only knew the wrath that would ensue if I didn't feed. "You have no idea just how hungry I am." My voice cracked as I spoke.

"Believe me. I know." Danny opened the mini refrigerator and took out two bags of blood. "Would you like them warmed up?" He raised his youthful-looking brow.

Normally I would prefer it warmed since the majority of my meals were hunted. The blood tasted better, almost like it was fresh. Today I was too tired. "No, but thank you. I'll take them both cold."

Damn it was good having my brother back. Searching for him had been something I never gave up on. Ciara supported my venture, but she didn't believe Danny had survived, since we'd never found as much as a trace of him anywhere.

Ahh…Ciara. I'd always blame myself for her death. Her life should've been natural, human. Had I been of sound mind when it happened, I wouldn't have changed her in the first place. The one thing I'd learned was not to force this on anyone if it could be helped, and I'd try to keep Libby in the dark for as long as it could be managed. Ciara's ruined life was enough, and I wouldn't let history repeat itself.

"How are you adjusting to being around Libby?"

I'd drained my second bag. The evidence of how I was adjusting seemed to equate to my literal thirst.

"I want her, Danny." The words slipped out like I'd just drank truth serum.

Danny's expression didn't change. He'd lived the dilemma that I now faced. "How's your self-control around her?"

"I don't know. Pretty good, I think. I can't really explain it." I wouldn't bite her again, but her blood wasn't something I wanted to conjure up after drinking two bags of human blood. Being around Libby or any human had its risks. There was no such thing as having complete self-control around her. I'd be foolish to entertain that notion.

"Do you plan on telling her?"

"No." Telling Libby I was a vampire was one of the last things I'd do. Neither Danny nor Shelby could push me to it—we'd all be exposed. Or worse, what if she left?

"You have to realize that she's going to get suspicious when you don't eat around her. She'll have questions."

I regarded Danny as I would a mirror. His expression looked the same as the one I wore. Our hair was different, as was our general styles, but so much about how we thought had to be on the same level. "I'll worry about that if it ever comes up. Maybe she'll never ask?"

"Maybe she won't. But you need to think of what you would tell her if she does. If she's anything like Shelby, then it's only a matter of time." Danny's hazel eyes bored into mine.

"I know…"

Nothing more needed to be said. I treaded on eggshells and knew it well.

Showering would be my last chore before I resigned myself to sleep. I climbed the stairs to the main level with more zeal than I had when I'd descended them. I pulled my clothes off and dropped them into a pile on the bathroom floor. I'd have to burn them. The scents they carried wouldn't wash out…not completely. I'd have to buy a new coat too. After I rested, I would return to Libby's side. Until then I wouldn't be good to anyone.

***

Libby

Squeaking floorboards woke me from a dead sleep. I opened my eyes to find Shelby creeping into my bedroom. Late-morning light danced on her skin as she paused at the side of my bed. I'd expected Liam, but he was nowhere to be seen.

As a part of Shelby's new normal, she looked great—better than great, really. Her glossy chestnut hair shone, and her skin was a shocking pale, but it all added up to a stunning look. She looked like a model without even trying. Not so long ago I was the friend men stared at, but now I expected Shelby drew her own attention, considering I couldn't even pull my eyes away from her. It didn't look like she was wearing makeup, but her tone was perfect, nor were there any blemishes. Her lips were the color of crushed berries, and her cheeks held a faint blush, even with tired-looking eyes.

"Did I wake you?" Shelby asked.

I opened my eyes wider while trying to adjust to the sunlight that streamed through the bedroom windows. "Yes, but I'm guessing that it's probably time to get up anyway?" I glanced at the clock that sat on my bedside table. It was already ten thirty! "Crap! I need to call Lillian." My heart pounded as if I'd be in big trouble for not reporting in with my boss. My work schedule wasn't enforced, but I couldn't miss work two days in a row without letting my boss know what was going on. Lillian wasn't paying me to lounge around my house.

"Okay, where's your phone? I'll call her if you want me to," Shelby offered.

"No, I'll call her. I think it's in my purse." Shelby turned and left to find my phone. She brought it to me moments later. Lillian's son, Christian, answered. I'd seen him answer the office phone before, and it was usually to help out while Lillian was away from her desk. As nice as he was, I didn't feel like faking causal talk.

"Hello, Christian, this is Libby." I lay back on the pillow and cradled the phone in my palm.

"Hey, Libby, what's up?" Christian's voice was warm. He always turned on the charm when he talked to me, as if we shared an intimate connection rather than an acquaintance-only vibe.

"Could you tell your mom that I need to take today off? I was sick yesterday too and feel a little better today, but I don't think I should be around anyone just yet." I coughed into the receiver for added effect.

"Is there anything you need? I could bring you anything you'd like to eat."

"Thanks, but I'll be fine. I've got everything I need here," I said in a way that I hoped would convey my desire to be alone. The food from his restaurant was beyond delicious, but the personal cost would be too great. Liam already had the market on taking care of me while I was recuperating. No more applicants needed.

Shelby raised her eyebrow and watched as I ended the conversation. "So what was that all about?"

"Nothing, believe me. My boss's son answered. I know that he likes me, maybe too much, but I'd never let anything happen."

"The whole business and pleasure thing?" Shelby sat on the empty side of the bed.

"Even if he wasn't my boss's son, it wouldn't work. It's just not like that—not for me it isn't." I sighed, hating how it felt to be housebound. Missing work sucked, but being resigned to my tiny town house was much worse.

"How's your hip feeling today? Liam said you'd hurt it."

I stretched and turned outward to relax my hips prior to trying to stand upright again. Oddly enough, there was no pain or stiffness. I wondered if it had fooled me again, like when I thought I could get out of the bathtub on my own, only to fall naked into Liam's arms.

"Yeah, I fell on it during the whole ordeal, but it actually feels fine now." I appreciated how Shelby hadn't lectured me off the bat, even though she always thought that she knew better. It was as if her moral compass pointed to true north, whereas mine sometimes pointed southward. I was more of a risk taker than she ever was and didn't need to hear how my actions could be dangerous. And considering I was still recovering from one of my most recent lessons.

Shelby walked over to my side of the bed and offered her hand for me to grab.

"I think you need house gloves. Your fingers are like ice."

"So I've been told."

Now that I was sitting on the side of the bed, nothing hurt at all. I remembered the bruise and wondered how it looked now that it should've set in. I pushed on the hip, but nothing was sore. Tentatively I raised my gown on the side and glanced down at it. Seeing nothing, I raised the gown higher until my hip was completely exposed except for the waistband of my panties.

"Looking for something?" Shelby focused her gaze on my hip. "Is that the hip that you fell on?" Her eyebrows drew together as she looked at my unbruised and healthy skin.

"Yeah, it was. I don't understand. It usually takes me a good week to heal a bruise, especially one that was so dark last night." I stared at my exposed skin and searched for a trace of discoloration, but there was none.

Shelby ran her hand over my hip. She looked like Sherlock Holmes, her eyes distant and speculative. "Did Liam give or do anything to help with the bruising?"

"Do anything?" His mouth had brushed over it, but it felt sensual, not medically driven. "Well, he kissed it, but that was all."

Shelby seemed strange, as if she was hiding something, but what? I was pretty sure she didn't want me to pursue Liam. Maybe she didn't think I was grown up enough for him? I had an extensive dating history, but Mr. Right still remained hidden. Maybe Liam was Mr. Right? "Do you want me to stay away from Liam for some reason?"

She hesitated. "No. Why would you think that?" Her voice carried a quiver in it. Was the answer in her quiver?

"I don't know. It just seems like you don't want me to be around him." She wasn't subtle at all.

Shelby gave a weak smile. "I just want you to be happy, and Liam's been through a lot, is all."

"I get it, but so have I." I couldn't even imagine the grief he must still feel, but there was something there with him that I couldn't explain. In some weird way, we seemed to complement each other. He was secure and steady, whereas I wasn't, and maybe we both needed more balance. I knew I did. Either way, this wasn't Shelby's call.

"I didn't want to intentionally make you feel like I wasn't supportive of you and Liam. I'm sorry." Shelby looked embarrassed. I couldn't tell when she was upset or nervous anymore. She used to wear her emotions on her face. It was like she'd grownup emotionally, while I still was quick to act on whatever came to mind.

"There's nothing to be sorry for." I smiled and tried to mean it. She was my best friend, and little things were too menial to come between us. I wondered where Liam was and when he would come back. I'd keep that question to myself though, at least for now.

Shelby made my bed as I dressed in the bathroom. It took a while to get my hair and makeup just right, even for a day spent inside. I dressed for comfort in yoga leggings and a long-sleeved purple V-neck shirt. I left the bathroom door open as I applied my makeup, and heard the chime of the doorbell. *Liam?*

Shelby zipped downstairs, returning minutes later. She poked her head into the bathroom.

"Well, you have lunch."

"What?" I asked, not understanding since neither of us had ordered takeout.

"Your friend Christian just brought you a crock of butternut squash soup and an asiago steak panini." She smirked. "He wanted to see you, but I told him that you were still in bed."

"Thank God you thought of that excuse." My stomach rumbled. "Well, that was really sweet. You'll have some too, right?"

"He likes you," Shelby said. "He wasn't bad looking either."

I rolled my eyes. "Regardless, there's no way I can eat it all." I followed Shelby downstairs. I held on to her shoulders because she was convinced that my hip would spasm, but I was fine. My arms were still stiff, but other than that, I had no complaints.

Shelby put the food on the kitchen table and insisted she wasn't hungry. I couldn't imagine why she'd be on a diet, as skinny as she was.

I sent Christian a thank-you text message for the lunch. It really had been a welcome surprise, no matter his intentions. Shelby thought that I was leading him on, but I wasn't going to be rude and not thank him.

After I ate, we sat in the living room with the TV on, like old times. We talked about the wedding—we'd soon need to try on dresses. She left in the early evening without once bringing up Sam. I was grateful for that and for her company. I joked that I had to get hurt for her to spend time with me, and I tried to play it off when she looked upset. I didn't want to hurt her. We really had a terrific friendship, and maybe I was a little too greedy when it came to her time. Either way, she was still my best friend. It bugged me that she wouldn't eat some lunch with me, not a single crumb, but after already having offended her diet, I wasn't going to push it any further, at least not today.

Chapter 3

Working Relationship

Libby

I'd waited, expecting to see Liam at some point in the day, but when the night darkened the sky, I was still alone. Being in an empty house didn't bother me, since I'd lived alone for years now, but I wasn't ready to be all by myself just yet.

Liam called after 9:00 p.m. and said he'd been told that I needed sleep more than I needed company, or at least that was Shelby's take on it. He didn't sound convinced but said he wouldn't want to upset Shelby on purpose. Her protectiveness was new and unwelcome. *Why did she think I'd want to be alone?* She treated me like I was fragile, but I guessed that was just a part of her new revamped self-esteem. I'd always wanted her to feel self-assured, but didn't realize that it would also make her more protective. She could've stayed with me if for some reason she wanted Liam to keep his distance.

I didn't sleep well at all—every sound prickled my senses. Sam knew where I lived…

Somehow I made it through the night, but I wouldn't be contained within the walls of the town house. I would go to see Shelby. I'd stopped by the printer's office days ago to pick up the wedding-invitation sample book, and I was supposed to go over the selections with Shelby on Thursday, but that hadn't happened. I didn't think about the invitations at all yesterday when I had Shelby around, so I had even more reason to visit.

The drive to Shelby's wasn't long, but the scenery was certainly different than what I could see out of my town house windows. The development I lived in sported similarly styled tan houses with small front yards. The backyards weren't much better, but they were fenced in, with room for entertaining. I'd thought about getting a dog for company, but that seemed like it'd be too much work, since I was gone for long stretches during the workweek.

As I drove toward Shelby's, the muted browns and leafless branches looked inviting. I didn't want to walk through it, but it was something different to behold other than office spaces or home interiors. A carpet of brown leaves covered the ground. I loved the town house, since I didn't have to worry about its exterior maintenance, but the unpredictable beauty of the forest had its own appeal.

The turn was near, but where was it? The driveway was almost hidden, which was why I'd slowed down to snail speed in search of the evasive turn. It'd tricked me the first time I drove here, but now I knew what to look for. The emerald mailbox poked through wispy trees. The vegetation around Danny's house was thick, which naturally gave the area an eternal curtain. Diffused light filtered through the trees, but it wasn't as intense as it'd been on the main road. In the distance was the footer to Liam's house. Shelby told me a little about the construction when I was last here, but Liam hadn't said a word about it—not that it would have come up after what he'd saved me from. Framing the walls would be next for Liam's house, though a massive amount of plywood would be needed for that job. The footer made it look like the house would be good sized.

With the wedding-invitation sample book under my arm, I walked to the front door. Brittle leaves crunched underfoot, but my hip glided without a hitch. I'd dressed casually in snake leggings and a tunic, with slate-gray heels. Shelby wouldn't baby me as much if I looked like I could take care of myself. I knocked twice, but there was no answer. I started to knock for a third time, but heard movements behind me.

"Libby?" Liam's husky voice startled me. The heavy sample book thudded to the porch.

He hadn't snuck up on me, but I couldn't fully settle myself down since the attack. I turned to face him with my hand on my chest. Liam picked up the book and held it out to me. Without thinking, I feigned falling into his arms as if I'd lost my balance. It was plausible, since my heels were thin and could throw anyone off balance. The only comfort I'd had in days was while I was in his arms.

"Libby?" Liam repeated. "Are you okay?"

I was okay now, and I made the impromptu decision to just go for it. I wanted him! Something about him fascinated me, or maybe I had a hero complex? I'd have to figure it out one way or another. I pulled his face down to meet mine and kissed him. I didn't know what my next move would be, but something changed in him too. At first he was careful with me and tried to pull away. I wouldn't let him go without force, which seemed to engage him further. Our teeth clicked together, and it was urgent for me to be with him, to own him, to be claimed by him. He lifted me so that my legs wrapped around his waist, and my arms clamped around his neck. My bad hip didn't even protest. I couldn't take my mouth off his. Everything else seemed second nature. He somehow opened the door and carried me to his bedroom. He hesitated, but I wouldn't back down from what I wanted.

"Libby, this isn't a good idea," he pleaded. "What about your hip?"

His mouth said one thing, but his body spurred me on. The metallic tang of blood was on my tongue, and I thought I must have cut my lip on his teeth. His body shuddered, so I ignored the blood. I lay on the bed…waiting for him.

"Are you on birth control?" he asked with hooded eyes.

I was on the pill, and most of the time I remembered to take it. "Yes," I panted. I couldn't tell if he'd heard me or not, but then he pulled my tunic over my head. With care he unbuttoned his shirt and dropped it on the floor. I watched as he methodically took off his pants. His underwear was bolder than I'd expected, but anything would've looked good on him. The boxer-briefs were silky, fitted, and deep green. My body ached for him and cramped in anticipation. He returned to me and pulled off my tights, which left me in my flame-orange bra and panties. He licked his lips and hovered over me. His mouth trailed kisses from behind my ear downward, but he stopped when his jaw touched my bra.

"Are you sure about this?"

His eyes met mine—there was no doubting my certainty.

I pushed my body against his. "You have no idea how sure I am."

Without any other prompting, he unhooked my bra and threw it on the floor. His tongue circled around one of my nipples, and then he pulled it into his mouth. I drew in a breath and arched my back to tighten his hold on me. He touch was unfamiliar but couldn't have been more in tune with my unvoiced pleas.

"You like that, do you?"

He eased my panties down past my hips, still taking care not to hurt my healed hip. I was naked again in his presence, but this time he didn't shield his eyes. He stiffened under the silky fabric that pushed against my thigh. He resisted his own pleasure as his finger explored the intricacies of my body. I moaned and dropped my legs open as he slowly pushed inside of me. He touched me like he was scared I'd break.

"You're not going to hurt me," I whispered.

He seemed to get the gist and pushed in with more force, while his other hand rested on the crest of my opening, rubbing in tiny circles. Normally it took a while for my climax to build, but between the thrusts of his long finger and the external stimulation, my body yielded to him. Gone were the apprehensions that usually clouded my mind during intimacy. With him I could let go in every way imaginable. I opened my legs wider, as if I could feel more by doing so. It was his cool mouth that set me over the edge. He'd bent over my open legs and pulled the skin of my sex into his mouth. His icy tongue brought on a shudder that rippled from somewhere deep inside. His mouth felt like he'd eaten ice cream, so cold, but soothing.

I spasmed as I screamed his name. "Oh…Liam!" My legs flailed as I outstretched my arms in undeniable bliss.

He didn't stop his pleasurable torture until I gasped for air. No orgasm had ever taken so much out of me.

He slid off his boxer-briefs, and his wide girth seemed to jump as it was freed. I'd never seen an uncircumcised man before. He was beautiful. His eyes bored into mine, and he looked possessed as he positioned himself over me. He didn't rush as he situated himself.

"Are you sure about this?" he asked again.

"Please," I begged as I pulled his hips closer to mine. There was a warning in his eyes that I ignored.

When he finally gave in and entered me, I cried. I stifled it as much as I could by biting my lip. *Am I ripping?* He pushed in with the gentlest of care, but his thickness pushed and expanded me deeper than I'd thought possible. And yet, he was holding back? I willed myself to relax as my body lubricated itself, and the pain diminished.

He'd tried to meet my eyes as I blinked away tears. I hadn't wanted him to see the pain. He pushed so deeply that my body trembled as undiscovered nerves endings were stimulated for the first time. A new sensation took over, and I wondered if it was me or him, but then his speed increased. He couldn't hold back any longer as his orgasm spilled itself inside of me, and his body relaxed. He rested on top of me for a few minutes before he pulled out. I was hollow without him inside of me. He pulled me to his chest and held me there.

"Are you okay?" His fingers stroked down my face and settled on my breast.

I was unable to speak with any sense after what'd happened, and so I just nodded my head once.

"I'm sorry I hurt you."

I looked at him. "Don't be. It felt right." My voice was weak.

"You have no idea..." His free hand wandered down between my legs, and he gently cupped me. "I'm sorry I made you bleed." *Oh crap!* It was official. I'd welcome death now if offered, but it turned out that it was not possible to die from embarrassment alone.

I looked down...shocked. There was blood on my thighs. I hadn't bled this much when I'd actually lost my virginity. "Since you broke me, you have to keep me." I didn't want him to feel guilty for this. I wished we'd done it in the dark. Then the evidence wouldn't have been discovered.

"Depend on it," he said.

I believed him. I hadn't had luck in other relationships, but Liam was different. I didn't know why, but I sensed he was worthy. I trusted him.

Liam

Libby's warm body curled into me, and minutes later her breathing slowed as she gave into sleep. Her lips were pursed like a tight flower, and she made a humming sound. I let her rest for a while, but we wouldn't have long. I rubbed down her back, feeling the curve of her spine and cool skin. I pulled the blanket over her, not wanting her to freeze to death.

I jostled her until she started stretching like a cat coming out of a nap. Her eyes flickered opened, dark lashes dancing.

"Would you like to shower off? I don't know how much time we have until Danny and Shelby return."

Libby pushed herself up into a sitting position. I cracked the door open to look out into the living room. "The coast is clear." We dashed into the bathroom wearing nothing at all. I heated the shower water to a temperature that would melt the goose bumps off her. I pulled Libby in behind me.

"Mmmm. This is divine." She stood directly under the showerhead. I rolled a bar of soap around inside of the folded washcloth until it was sudsy and lathered Libby's body all while taking care to rinse off all the blood that remained from our encounter. It was bad enough that I had to endure its sweet scent, but if Shelby and Danny picked up on its fragrance, it'd be apparent what we'd done.

After the shower, Libby and I dressed all while trying to look like normal and sane people. I scrambled to change the bed linens and threw the dirty ones in the washer, not that the smell of blood would be entirely washed away. My standard laundry detergent was fragrance-free, but today I used Shelby's Gain Hawaiian aloha fragrance.

I handed Libby a mug of steaming chamomile tea with honey, as she needed something to take the edge off, while I sipped on black coffee. We sat on the porch since both of us needed some kind of distraction. The air was cool, but a few minutes outside wouldn't hurt Libby, not with the warm mug in her hands. Hiding my attraction was pointless now, and I doubted that it would convince anyone if I even attempted it, but our physical union was premature. Danny had been smarter when it came to Shelby and hadn't gone there, but I couldn't wait, not when Libby was so insistent.

She wouldn't know how deep our bond was now. Sex wasn't a casual act like it could be with humans—far from it. We didn't only mate for pleasure or procreation, but it was how we bonded as a couple...now we were something more than friends or even family.

During sex, vampires secreted hormones that bonded one to the other. Since Libby was human, she wouldn't have those type of hormones but would reciprocate with feelings of connection. The hormones were released with every sexual encounter, which reinforced a couple's connection. Without the release of the hormone, I doubt that Ciara and I would have lasted past her initial change, much less as long as we endured. Not that a hormone could work if love wasn't there to begin with. One thing I'd noticed was how different couples were affected by the hormone—some with intense attachment, while others were volatile. The mutation of vampirism was always about survival, and when we had stable mates, then we were more likely to survive and continue with our way of life.

The look in Libby's eyes had changed with our attachment. I'd known that she'd liked me before, but now she was in need of a constant connection. Small displays of affection were enough to satisfy her, so I held her as much as possible or held her hand. I was affected too—her scent was hypnotic, her beauty unparalleled. *Love* couldn't describe my flooding emotions.

Libby seemed like someone who was confident, but I knew it was a mask. She was vulnerable, just like me. She didn't want to let anyone too close to her emotionally, and so she'd always armored herself. She'd let others have her body, while her mind remained locked away, hidden. We shared a trust that bared all, except for what I really was. How could she understand? My kind should have only existed in fairy tales, not real life. For now, I had to keep quiet and hope she'd never ask. We went back inside once our mugs were drained. She seemed like she could be hot tempered, though temperament alone couldn't keep her warm.

"What do you think they'll say?" Libby sat on the sofa and tried to look casual, but her pulse quickened as she spoke.

"Say about what?" I asked as I sat down beside her. I'd been pacing the room and thought I was the root of her anxiety.

She looked down, avoiding my gaze. "About us."

"What can they say?" I hadn't planned on telling Shelby or Danny yet, but I wasn't going to torture

Libby either. She'd known that Shelby didn't want us together. I wondered if she thought both Shelby and Danny were against us.

"Well…" She sighed. "Shelby doesn't want us to be together, and I'm guessing that Danny probably feels the same way."

"She'll come around, and Danny is already supportive." Danny had as much as thrown me at Libby in the hope of bringing me back from figurative death.

Libby wiped at her eyes. This upset her more than I could understand.

"I didn't think Danny liked me."

I cringed and realized just how perceptive she was. Danny wasn't Libby's biggest fan—at least, he wasn't initially. The truth was, Libby and Danny were very different people on the surface. He'd started to come around when he wanted to give me a distraction. He seemed to even like her a little now.

"He just takes a while to warm up to new people." I lifted her chin so that her eyes met mine. "Besides, who wouldn't like you?"

Libby's cheeks flushed to a deep crimson. If she was going to have reactions like this, then I'd need to feed again soon. I'd never be able to keep my secret safe if her blood called to me as much as it did, though I'd hurt myself before I'd ever think of taking her blood. Some vampire couples, and even vampire/human couples, would bite for sexual arousal as a way to heighten intensity. The thought of it made my pants feel tighter as I imagined making love to Libby and biting her at climax. She'd never understand though, and it would always be too risky.

"So when do you think they'll be home?" She sounded like she wanted to let Shelby and Danny know about us as soon as she could. Tension lines marred her perfect forehead as she sat in worry.

Shelby may not like the idea of us together, but what could she do about it? "I think they'll be home soon." They'd left early in the morning to hunt. They'd driven down to Virginia, where there was a low human population and where Shelby could tune in to her instincts. Not that there was a greater variety of prey there, but at least Shelby wouldn't have the home advantage. A new environment would help to develop her skills and make her a sharper hunter. None of us fed off humans, even though our bodies digested human blood the easiest. Some drank bagged human blood, but never from the vein, at least not anymore. Had I partaken on human blood as a staple of my diet, there would be no way I could be in Libby's company, not to mention the intimacy we'd shared.

Danny and Shelby were close now. Hair prickled on the back of my neck as I recognized their familiar energy getting closer by the second. I subconsciously begged Shelby to keep her cool and prayed that it might somehow all be all right. She would have to trust me with her friend because there was no other way around it.

Libby

"Did you hear that?" Liam asked.

"Do I hear what?"

"They're home."

Liam's frigid fingers twined in mine. Was I the only person who still had warms hands? Neither

Shelby nor Liam did, that was certain. I blew out, but my jitters remained. Shelby entered, followed by Danny. When Shelby's eyes rested on me, her face went from happy to something I couldn't pinpoint. She stared at my hand that was still weaved in Liam's. Danny seemed unfazed and continued into the house without preamble. Maybe Liam was right about Danny approving of me.

"How was your ride?" I asked Shelby. I couldn't stand the silence and tension that filled the air. Liam said that they'd gone for a day trip somewhere, only now I wondered, where to?

"Fine…" She looked me in the eye and smiled. It looked forced, but at least she wasn't as hostile as she first seemed.

"I brought the wedding-invitation sample book over. I thought that you might want to look at it with me?" Liam let go of my hand, and I lifted the book from the coffee table. Danny asked Liam to join him in the basement, though Liam assured me that he'd be back soon. Shelby took his place on the sofa as I flipped through the pages. My heart pounded, and part of me wondered if Shelby could tell what I'd done. I usually told her this kind of secret without any hesitation, but she didn't want me anywhere near Liam as it was. I didn't regret what we'd done and didn't need Shelby's approval.

"That one is nice." Shelby pointed to an invitation that was on heavy ivory card stock. The font was in burgundy and was accented with gold foil. It'd be perfect for her Christmas wedding. So we'd dance around the subject first? Not that I minded.

"I like it too. It's perfect." I traced my finger over the font. The paper was of good quality. Nothing about it looked cheap.

"It's not too cliché?"

"Not at all. The colors and style are what you wanted."

We thumbed through the remainder of the book just to be sure that the first choice was the right one. There were a couple other styles that Shelby liked, but nothing that was as fitting as the wintery ivory sample. I marked the page with a Post-it note. Shelby would have to return the sample book and place the order, though her mom would likely be the one to pay for it. I offered to drop the book by her mother's house, but Shelby declined. She said that she was going to see her mom sometime this week and would want her mother's input before it was finalized.

We sat and talked, but I couldn't shake the judgment that seemed directed toward me. I didn't want to disappoint Shelby, but at the same time there was no way I'd refuse Liam just to gain her approval. *What was her deal?*

"So, about the white elephant in the room?" Shelby said.

"About that…" I didn't know how much she knew, and I wasn't going to divulge anything unless necessary.

"So you're with Liam now? Officially, I mean?" Shelby straightened her posture as she awaited my answer.

I didn't know how to soften it or why I even needed to, when it was something I wanted. "Yes, we're together." I held her gaze for as long as I could before looking down at the invitation book. She wasn't a pushover anymore…

"So are you sure you two are compatible? I mean, he's seriously reserved. Once he's committed, that's it for him." Her tone was even, and her meaning was clear. She didn't want me to mess things up like I had in every other relationship. She couldn't see the difference in Liam and the other men I'd dated. Liam was special.

"I'm sure about Liam. I feel like I can trust him, and there's a connection between us. It's different." My hands moved as I spoke, as if I could somehow show Shelby how alive I was with him.

She looked speculative, but she didn't elaborate on her thoughts. "Okay then."

"So we're okay?" She didn't seem okay, but maybe she'd need more time for it to sink in.

"Of course we are."

Her words fell flat, but what she said would have to be enough for now.

The stairs creaked as Liam and Danny emerged from the basement. Was Danny actually smiling at me? Well, at least someone was happy for Liam and me.

"I understand that we'll be seeing you around a little more frequently," Danny said with a warm smile. His teeth were as pristine as Liam's. I'd have to ask Liam about his parents sometime. With teeth that good in the family, they had to be dentists.

I wasn't sure how to answer without sounding ridiculous, and I tried to keep my cool. "Yeah. That is, if you don't mind."

"You're always welcome here. Besides, I think Shelby's missed having you around." Danny's gaze shifted to Shelby.

I looked in Shelby's direction too. She wasn't frowning, but she wasn't wishing us well either. What was her objection? *Geesh!* She should have my back on this. I wasn't walking into this relationship blindly. I knew we'd both have to work at it to make it successful. We both could get hurt in the process, but that was our business.

"Have you asked her yet?" Danny said to Liam. "She'll steer you in the right direction." Danny nudged Liam in his ribs.

Liam sat down beside me to reclaim his spot as Shelby and Danny disappeared into the office with the excuse that they needed to catch up on work.

"I was wondering if you'd like to help me by doing my interior design."

He seemed reluctant to ask for help, but then again he might have been scared away by how I'd decorated my town house with bold patterns and colors. "I'd love to help you."

"I'd go through the design company that you work for, of course. That way you'd be given the time to spend with me, and a commission," Liam said, like he'd have to convince me to be around him more often.

"We can start on Monday. I'll have to let my boss know, and I'll bring the paperwork over to get you under contract." My touch and influence would be a part of his house now. We were making memories together already.

"So the house doesn't have to be completed before we begin?"

He was so naive.

"Of course not. Besides, we'll want to order certain things before the house is completed. That way we'll have everything we need to get it installed on time. You won't have to settle for whatever is available locally." Custom items could take months. Time was never of the essence when building a house.

"You're the pro. It looks like I'm in good hands." He drew closer and bent to whisper in my ear. "So are you and Shelby okay now?" He seemed to know how delicate my healing friendship was with her. More importantly, he worried about my feelings.

I matched his whisper, not wanting Shelby to overhear the conversation. "I think so. She worries that I'll do something rash to hurt you."

His conspiring tone didn't alter. "She may say that she's worried about you hurting me, but I think you know the truth. She'll always be protective of you. You're her best friend."

"Why does she think that I need protecting?" My voice crescendoed. I cleared my throat and resumed the whisper. "What does she think is going to happen then?"

His eyes grew serious, but he tried to maintain the same level of intimacy that ran through our conversation. "I guess it's the fact that no one is perfect. Maybe she thinks that once you really get to know me, you'll change your mind?"

The thought of being without him stirred my stomach to the point of nausea. "There's nothing you can say that's going to change how I feel about you, Liam." Unwelcome tears hung in my lashes. Maybe I was giving away too much of myself? I couldn't tell, having never felt this way about another person before. I wanted him to know his value in my life—it seemed important somehow.

"The thing is…" He paused for a moment before he spoke again. "It doesn't matter if you hurt or leave me. I'd prefer that you didn't, but I won't have you with me just to protect my feelings. I want to take each day as it comes and enjoy you for as long as you'll allow me that privilege."

His words were heavy and pained. I didn't want him to live only for today. I could promise him more than that, but at the same time I didn't want to sound pathetic. "I won't hurt you."

"Maybe not, but I want you to know in your heart that I won't hold you responsible if you do."

We sat in silence for a while. I didn't know what else to say, but for once I felt like the man I loved was in my grasp, and he was there by choice. Maybe that was all he meant, that we'd be together by choice only. I couldn't image choosing any different, not after having a taste of him.

***

Liam

Libby left just after breakfast. She'd stayed over, and I didn't want her to go. How could she understand? She was fragile, and I'd already lost a mate that was almost bulletproof. Greed for Libby clouded my judgment, but letting her out was vital to our relationship if it was going to continue. I had to feed, and that was a vice that was cutting deeper into my daily routine. Libby wasn't a morning person, so when she finally awoke, of course I'd already eaten. I'd prepared her pancakes and bacon. She ate and raved about my cooking. Maybe she wouldn't reciprocate the gesture…my dietary preferences wouldn't be in a cookbook.

Shelby was groggy and looked annoyed when she'd seen Libby. I'd hoped that the tension would fizzle out.

Libby had picked up on Shelby's mood and remarked under her breath that she was just hungry. Libby practically forced a piece of toast down Shelby's throat before it was over. *What a disaster…*

Libby left after that, saying she needed to cool down. Shelby went back upstairs and regurgitated the dry toast.

I heard footsteps and looked to see Danny coming downstairs. Tension sullied his face as he carried wet towels to the laundry room.

"How is she?" I asked.

"She'll be fine after she sleeps it off," Danny said. He threw the towels in the hamper and sat down beside me at the kitchen counter.

"I don't know what else to do. I know that Libby is going to keep insisting on things that she can't understand," I said. She was stubborn and feisty. Backing down wasn't in her nature.

Danny raked his fingers through his hair, pushing back the dark strands. "Your guess is as good as mine."

"The thing is, they're friends. On one hand, Shelby is trying to protect Libby from what we are.

On the other hand, Libby is clueless, and it's for the best she remain that way." I paused. "I can't cut things off with her either..." She'd be safer—heck, we'd all be safer if I could give her up, but that wasn't an option.

"I don't know what to tell you. If you'd asked me what to do before Shelby came along, then I'd tell you to let her go. Now I know that it's a choice you can't make. It's already decided. Besides, you two have something." Danny patted my back. It was supposed to be a soothing gesture, but my fate with Libby was unsettling. Exposure could be the end of us.

I cleared my throat. "True. I just wish it wasn't so complicated." I tried not to complain, because Libby was the best thing I could be blessed with, but how could it last?

"It's going to be complicated for a while. I don't know how it will all work out in the end, but you can't give up. You've changed. I see how you look at her. You need her."

I nodded but had no solution. I could make it work on a superficial level at least, but I wanted to be all in with her. I loved her.

"Can you answer a question for me though?" Danny looked confused but curious.

"What is it?"

"Were you and Libby intimate?" Danny's cheeks flushed scarlet.

My face grew hotter too. There was no point in lying. "We were."

"How is that even possible? Weren't you afraid of hurting her?" Danny hadn't touched Shelby when she was human. He didn't know what he'd missed.

"I was terrified, but at the same time I knew I wouldn't hurt her...I couldn't hurt her."

"But you still crave her blood?" Danny's eyes widened with interest.

"Then there's that. If I were to bite her while we made love, she would probably have an anxiety attack. But I craved it nonetheless." I looked down as I spoke, trying to avoid the judgment that remained there, but then met his accepting gaze.

"I'm sure she would." Danny smiled. "Was that something you did with Ciara?"

"Sometimes, but she didn't really like to experiment."

"I think Shelby wants to, but part of me still believes that I'd hurt her. It's irrational, I know."

"Give it time."

Danny shook his head. "Back to you and Libby. She's on birth control, isn't she?" Danny sounded like the responsible big brother he'd been two hundred years ago. The topic would've been different, but still...

"She said that she's on the pill." I'd worried about the repercussions of unprotected sex with a human. We couldn't pass our mutation on through sex, or any illnesses for that matter, but there was always the risk of pregnancy...

"Did she ask about STDs?"

"No, she didn't, but she's reckless...almost dangerous." I'd been adamant that she continue taking her birth control pills. There was something I could unintentionally give her still, though it wasn't a common occurrence…a baby. Female vampires were infertile, but a male vampire could still spawn life. It rarely happened, and I'd never seen its result. Most vampires bonded with other vampires. Occasionally male vampires would go after humans for sex only. Most of the time those sex-driven relationships ended up with death for the human. The pregnancy story could be mythical, but just in case, Libby would remain on the pill.

"Just be careful. It's risky." Danny looked as worried as I felt.

In one small way Libby had protection, and that was Shelby. She'd kill me if I ever hurt Libby, not that I could blame her. "I'll try…"

"It's just good to have you back."

What he meant was that it was good that I was back and engageable, unlike the walking corpse I had been after I'd lost Ciara.

We both turned at the sounds coming from upstairs.

"I better go and check on her." Danny patted me on the shoulder before ascending the stairs.

"Good luck with that!"

A sick vampire was a lot like a bear awoken from hibernation. We tended to be intolerant to any degree of physical discomfort. Our digestive systems were only capable of handling a few things, all of which were liquid. Blood was the only thing we fed on and grew strength from, but we could also tolerate red wine, coffee, and water. Our palates weren't designed for variety, but we appreciated the bouquet that was found in both blood and wine. Drinking wine helped us to fit into society, or at least helped to disguise our malady. Just how much longer could I get by with only coffee, wine, or water in front of Libby?

Danny was lucky. He had it all. Shelby had also been a human when they met, and Danny helped her transition into a vampire to save her life, and she didn't resent him for that choice—she welcomed it.

Chapter 4

Design

Libby

Sleep was fitful and lonelier than I'd prefer. But I'd be a good sport about it for now. As much as I wanted to stay with Liam again, or have him stay here, we weren't there yet. Evidently the concept of too much of a good thing existed, so for now I'd try and keep things light. I had to get to the office to let my boss know about Liam's project before she assigned me to another design. Lillian didn't mind when I did work for family or friends, and as a bonus it brought in more clients, but these projects couldn't interfere with jobs already planned.

Liam, bless his heart, had come over to check on me last night after the whole Shelby incident. It wasn't a big deal, just Shelby being stubborn as usual, but for some reason he thought I'd be upset. The whole evening had been eaten up with the minor drama that left us with no time for ourselves as a couple. Most men that I'd shared intimacy with weren't easy to talk to, but that wasn't the case with Liam. He had worthwhile opinions—he wasn't only a handsome face. Being with him in any way made the time slip by at a cheetah's speed.

Liam didn't understand the relationship I shared with Shelby, sisterly in some ways. Disputes with Shelby would have to be settled between the two of us, like we'd done a million times before. What I couldn't understand was why Danny hadn't addressed Shelby's obvious eating disorder. Not that Shelby looked sick, but she was so thin that it couldn't be healthy. To top it off, I never saw her eating anymore. Liam tried to dismiss it, but I couldn't let Shelby starve herself. Maybe making her eat wasn't the answer, but she wouldn't see my reasoning any other way. Besides, it would only get worse if nothing was done. She didn't see the problem, and it'd take someone like Danny or her mom to really break through her thick head.

Eight o'clock beamed from my dashboard as I pulled into my parking space. The office wasn't open to the public yet, but Lillian was already inside. Her shiny BMW was parked next to her son's car. I'd have to thank him for the food he brought me when I was...sick. I grabbed my purse, wiped lipstick off my teeth that I'd spotted in the mirror, and headed inside.

Christian was perched on my desk as if he'd been waiting for me. *Great.* On any other day I'd still be home at this time. He stood as I neared, and on my desk sat an arrangement of spring flowers. I stared at it, willing it to disappear. So it was going to be like that, was it? Lillian was in her office with the door shut. She was also in on the plan.

"How are you feeling today?" Christian asked. Concern edged his voice. He'd slicked back his blond hair and wore a fitted black waffle-knit thermal shirt and jeans. He was attractive, but I couldn't lead him on any longer. *Out with it.*

"Much better, thanks. The panini and soup you sent over the other day were wonderful." He'd brought the food over himself, but that acknowledgment would've been too personal. The flowers taunted me. Darn, this wasn't going to be easy.

Christian pulled the card out of its forked holder and handed me the sealed envelope. So ignoring it wasn't going to make it go away? I read it while Christian stared at me with a nervous expression on his face.

The card read, *I'd like to keep you warm the next time you're sick. Yours, C.* Nausea bubbled in my stomach. I cleared my throat and tried to think of something to say to soften the blow. This had to end. Not telling him outright would be inhumane. "That's really sweet, but…" My voice cracked, and I could already see the disappointment in his drooping smile.

"You know we'd make a good pair," he said, as if to prevent me from delivering the final blow.

"I've no doubt of that, Christian. Really, I know that you're a good guy. You'd make any woman happy," I rambled.

"But?" He wasn't going to let me off without perfect clarity.

"I'm seeing someone," I said in a rush.

"Oh, I'm sorry then." Christian brushed his hands over his shirt as if to straighten wrinkles from his put-together attire. His cheeks were red, as if someone had slapped both sides of his face.

"No, it was such a sweet gesture. Thank you…" I gushed. The look in his eyes was heartbreaking. I wasn't a softy, but Christian was a really good guy. I didn't want to be the cause of his pain.

"I've got to get going. Maybe I'll see you around." He turned and was out the door before I could say another word. He didn't even tell his mother good-bye.

After Christian left, I put the card back into the envelope, figuring I'd dispose of it at home. I couldn't leave it here to be read by his mother. Lillian liked me, but hurting her only child's feelings would leave a bad taste in her mouth, not that I could blame her. I powered on my computer and entered Liam's information into the system and assigned myself as his personal designer.

Lillian came out of her office just after nine to unlock the front door. Her face was a mask. Of course she'd already talked to Christian.

"I see you've got a client?" Lillian stood in front of my desk, looking severe but not hostile.

"Yes. I'm planning on going by there today with some design ideas," I said in a cheerful voice.

"That's probably a good idea." Her words were apt, but her tone was off.

"Look… Lillian, Mrs. Spencer."

Her expression shifted when I called her Mrs. Spencer.

"I didn't mean to upset Christian. You know how much I love working here, and I'd never want to hurt his feelings or upset you."

"He'll be okay. It's just that he's had his eye on you for a while. It's taken a lot of encouragement for him to talk to you…" Lillian said in a gentler timbre.

"I'm sure it did. But he's more like a brother to me. I think that I've known him for too long to see him in any other way." I tried to sound genuine, which I was, but I didn't want to bring up the fact that it would be awkward dating my boss's son. She had to know that, right?

"I understand, Libby. Maybe if you know of any nice girls, you would let me know. You've seen the bolder side of him. Had he not known you for as long as he had, he wouldn't have even approached you." Her smile warmed her face—all was forgiven.

"I can think of one off the top of my head." My cousin Sarah. She was single and lived with a roommate in Salisbury. She was pretty but gawky, with her oversized ears and long, plain hair. She was shy as Christian and just as sweet. She hadn't ever had a real boyfriend, and she was twenty-four years old.

"Really?" Lillian's eyebrows rose.

"My cousin Sarah. She looks a lot like me but is more toned down. Their biggest obstacle would be getting to know each other, because she's very quiet too."

"Maybe you could call her and set something up? He's free Friday evening or Saturday afternoon." It was odd how well she knew her son's schedule, but he was a mama's boy. Yet another reason why we would never have worked out.

"Yeah, I'll call her and see when she's free." I knew Christian would go for her and wondered if maybe they should meet over lunch, or maybe doing some sort of activity, just to get them talking.

I called Sarah before I left the office to see if she would be available. She was nervous to commit to a setup that I'd arranged. I told her about Christian, and the fact that he was my boss's son seemed to seal the deal, and she finally warmed up to the idea. Christian wasn't a reject, and in general, he was a catch, just not my type. The initial date was set for Saturday afternoon at the roller-skating park in Salisbury.

From the way Lillian spoke, Christian had already forgiven me.

***

This time Danny's driveway didn't elude me. I could've driven by it a thousand times before and not known it was even there, but now the mailbox caught my eye. Things were still up in the air between Shelby and me, so conversation would be forced, if she even showed her face. Should I apologize for something that I didn't really feel like I needed to apologize for? Perhaps forcing jellied toast down her throat was a little extreme, even for me. She'd have to get over it though. She'd always liked grape jelly, so she shouldn't have protested so much to begin with.

I grabbed more than I could carry, looking like a pirate with his arms full of booty, and walked toward the house. I had paint swatches, fabric samples, and books filled with cabinet styles from five different companies. In retrospect I should've made two trips to the car. Liam said that he'd picked out flooring already, which in a way would make my job easier. With the flooring in mind, other details would all have to match it. I struggled to the door and managed to knock at it with my foot. My knocking was faint but persistent. I didn't want to scuff the toe of my knee-high leather boots, but I'd start dropping things if the door wasn't opened soon. Someone had heard me, and the door opened. Danny smiled as he took on my burden. He led me in and set the samples down on the kitchen table.

"It looks like you'll be busy today. I'll get Liam for you." Danny disappeared down to the basement but returned moments later with Liam trailing him.

"We'll be in the office if you need me or Shelby."

"Thank you, Danny!" Though I couldn't tell if he'd heard me, as he'd closed his office door behind him. I looked at Liam, and my cheeks burned. *What was this?* Today his eyes were more green than brown. The thing about hazel eyes that I loved was their ability to shift from green to brown and sometimes to a yellowish color. My eyes were blue, and I never noticed any variation in them. His haphazard caramel hair stuck up all over the place, but on him it was charming. He was a gorgeous man and unlike anyone I'd ever known, with the exception of his brother. They favored one another in a way that they looked more like twins rather than regular siblings. They weren't identical, but there were enough similarities between the two to make that assumption.

"So I take it that you're planning on doing some work today then?" Liam's mischievous eyes crinkled at the sides, as if *other* arrangements could be organized.

"That's the plan." I aligned the sample books and pulled out the paint swatches. I needed to know where to start, and it was usually best to begin with a color palate. "What's the building timeline?" I looked down, engrossed in finding the section I wanted. He stood behind my chair but bent over as he looked at the swatches in my hand. His cool breath tickled my neck. My head began to swim…I was intoxicated by him.

"The foundation is complete, and the construction should be finished no later than the end of June to the beginning of July. So four more months, tops." He paused. "Please, no hot-pink walls," he whispered into my ear.

He kissed the side of my neck as my breathing caught in my throat. Did he know what he did to me? "I didn't think you were a fan of pink, so earthier tones?" I tried to keep my composure. He kissed my jawline.

"I guess so, but I'd like to see all of my options first." The sound of his voice was clear, as if he was unfazed by the havoc that he had caused. He sat down in the chair beside me and seemed ready to get to work.

"We'll need a color palate, which could be used to accent furniture or painted onto drywall." Once he was far enough away from me, but still sitting to my side, my head normalized. The haze that I'd been under moments before cleared.

"Oh, and no zebra sofas either."

"Is there anything you actually like about my town house?" I'd designed it to my own taste and could understand why a man might not be at home there, but I still wanted him to like what I liked.

"Of course there is." His grin widened.

"And that is?"

"Well, you live there, don't you?"

So I was his favorite thing at my town house…

"I could say the same about this house, you know." The design wasn't bad at Danny's. It had a lot of upscale touches like hardwoods, travertine tile, and granite counters, but no pops of color.

"I'm sure it's too monotone for you. Your color choices are as lively as you are." His hand brushed mine as I moved the color swatches in front of him. Liam's eyes sparkled at me, like he was hungry, maybe even ravenous, but not for food. Too bad that Danny and Shelby were here. I'd like to see what that look in his eyes was all about… Instead, I moved on to the book on cabinets. The options had low and high ranges. It all came down to what Liam wanted to spend and the style he desired. I couldn't even guess his budget, since he worked as a freelance business consultant.

"Have you got a certain budget to work with for this design?" I stared down at the cabinet book. I kept my cool better when I didn't look straight at him or touch him.

"I don't have a budget." He laughed as he spoke, as if spending was of no consequence for him.

"What?" I looked up to meet his gaze.

"What I meant to say is that money isn't a problem for me. I'll pay whatever it costs."

"I'm not sure if you know what you're saying. Custom cabinets can cost as much as fifty thousand dollars." Maybe he didn't know how expensive it could get?

His expression didn't change. "That isn't a problem."

"So, I'm hearing that you have an unlimited budget?" *Whoa!*

"That's right. I want a house that is comfortable but also sturdy. I want to buy things that last the test of time. Also, I'd like it to be a home that you would feel comfortable in too."

My heart fluttered. Part of me hoped that I would be able to leave my stamp on his house as a way to keep me on his mind. I hadn't considered the possibility that he would actually want me around long term. "I would like that too," I confessed in a whisper.

Work with Liam flew by without any sense of time passing. He made decisions without overthinking them. He decided on custom wood cabinets for both the kitchen and bathrooms. He wanted to keep things consistent throughout, and he chose a mocha-colored cabinet that was detailed enough to make up for the lack of vivid color that I liked. My preference would've been for white or robin's egg–colored cabinets, but they wouldn't match the theme of a log house and would have looked ridiculous. Even though we still needed to make decisions on countertops, furniture, and window treatments, we'd accomplished a lot for one day. My stomach growled, and I blushed as I looked at the clock. Just past three o'clock. *I'd forgotten to eat?*

"You must be hungry. I can't believe I forgot to feed you."

He'd forgotten to feed me? Was I a pet fish? "Don't worry about it. I'll get something when I get home." My fingers shook as I looked through the books, and I hoped he wouldn't notice, but my stomach growled again.

"No, you've got to eat. Obviously you're hungry." Liam stood up and went to the refrigerator.

I could see him from where I sat at the kitchen table. I wasn't going to fight him on this. I was hungry.

"Do you like grilled cheese sandwiches?"

"Yes."

"What kind of cheese would you like? We have cheddar, Swiss, and American."

"Cheddar would be great." I watched as he heated up the cast-iron skillet on the gas range. The first sandwich he made was a failure, completely blackened on one side. The next time, though, the sandwich was golden on each side. I waited for it to cool a little but ate it while it was still hot. He hadn't asked me, but minutes later he produced another sandwich. "Aren't you hungry too?" I asked. He hadn't eaten while I'd been with him.

"No, I'm lactose intolerant. I'll get something later."

I wasn't going to turn the sandwich down, but who liked eating alone? "Wouldn't you like to eat with me?" I couldn't understand it. Was this whole house against nourishment?

"I'm really not hungry. I had a heavy breakfast, and I'm still full. Sorry, Libby." He shrugged but then cleaned up the mess.

I ate like I was starving and then thanked him for feeding me. Sometimes he seemed like my guardian, the way he tried to take care of me. I didn't mind it, but at the same time I wanted to be more for him too. When I left, I wondered why Shelby hadn't come out at all to see me, and worried that she was still upset.

So mending fences would take longer this time than it had in the past?

***

Liam

Libby had gone back to her office to put in what orders she could enter at this point. I found my way around the build site. It was beginning to look more like a house. Basic walls had been put up today, so I could really see how each area would be divided. I could imagine Libby at the kitchen counter, or at least where it would be once it arrived. Every room had a hint of her in it, as if she was a part of the foundation itself. She'd be the one to make it a home with her designs, not just a place to exist. I looked back as I left. It was still hard to believe that it would be mine. The walk back to Danny's was a short one. We'd be close enough, but not on top of one another. A little separation was a good thing when it came to family. Pocomoke was my home now, and for once it felt right.

Danny's house seemed as if it'd been hollowed out now that Libby was gone. I wasn't alone. Danny and Shelby worked in the office with the door closed. But Libby's absence drowned out every other presence. The draw that pulled me to her wasn't something I could verbalize this early on, especially to a human. I'd see her later though, no doubt about it.

Shelby's avoidance of Libby only incited tension. I might have forgotten to feed Libby, but even I sensed that Shelby keeping to the office all day would've been interpreted as odd. Shelby had to know that, right? It wasn't so long ago that she was human… Even though I didn't eat in front of Libby, I did go into the restroom once to give her the illusion of me being normal. This ruse was getting old, even this early on, but still, she couldn't know the truth. I sat back down at the kitchen table for a while and looked at the samples that I'd picked. Libby had taken the reject pile to her office. She said that my cabinet order wouldn't go in until we knew just what we needed, with its proper dimensions. I had her email the requests to the contractors. The head contractor had emailed back saying the measurements would be sent to Libby directly within twenty-four hours.

Forty minutes after Libby left, Danny's office door opened. He emerged and nodded in my direction as he climbed the stairs. Shelby followed after Danny, her head down, avoiding my gaze. Instead of going after Danny, Shelby sat down in Libby's empty chair.

"How was Libby today?" Her tone was genuine but nervous.

"She's fine, but I'm sure she found it odd how you didn't come out to use the restroom or eat anything again." I hadn't been a human in two hundred years, but acting human wasn't something I'd forgotten. My impersonation wasn't seamless but was plausible in most situations.

"That's what Danny said too." Shelby focused her eyes on the table. Her cheeks flushed, and red blotches spotted her neck.

"You should've listened to him." My tone was harsh, but she'd have to learn somehow. Danny loved her, and I did too, like she was family, but Danny needed to be more direct with her. Shelby had to learn the dos and don'ts of vampirism. One key concept it took to be a good vampire was the ability to blend in with humans.

"I'll go see her tomorrow." Her face crinkled, as if faking human was her bane.

"I hope that you don't look like that when you go. That face would scare her to death." I laughed as I remembered how I'd once tried to fit in to society. Ciara was there to help me, but she was just as bad as I was at that point. Only time and practice helped.

"I'll be fine." Shelby ran her hands through her hair. It bounced back into place looking luminous and styled.

"I'm sure you will be."

I took a walk after talking with Shelby. The sun was setting, and the tree line was almost pure black. Movement was one of the only things that calmed my nerves. Shelby hadn't meant to be as conspicuous as she had, but nonetheless she put off a strange vibe. She'd try to come off as normal, but how convincing could she be? Being a new vampire had its own challenges, what with the new tasks of hunting, feeding, and adapting to amped-up senses, which meant trying to act human wasn't high on the list of to-dos as a vampire, but it mattered if you lived among humans.

I knocked on Libby's front door just after six. I'd bought a bottle of water and had already opened it and poured half of it out to look like I'd drank it. I could drink water without getting sick, but it had zero appeal.

Libby's SUV rested in its parking space, and a faint light filtered through the curtains of the town house. I knocked again and noticed the drapes move as Libby's face peered through a small slit of curtain. The door clicked as the latch gave way, and the door opened inward. She'd restrained herself at Danny's, and now I was greeted as she bounded into my arms. If I were human, I would have been pushed back by her impact.

"Did you miss me?"

She wouldn't have had time to really miss me, though my heart ached without her near.

"I missed being close to you. I had to behave at Danny's."

I carried her inside, all while shutting and relatching the door.

"You don't have to be on your very best behavior there, do you?"

Just how hard had she fallen?

"Of course I do."

Her cheeks reddened as her pulse echoed in my ears.

The way her body smelled, and her proximity, weakened my resolve. I wanted to control myself around her and treat her like she deserved. The animal desire inside wouldn't allow that though. For some reason I couldn't understand, my attraction to her had nothing to do with her blood. It didn't even call to me like it would with another human. Her blood was a separate entity in some ways. I wouldn't turn down a taste of it, but never in malice. She clung to me, with her legs wrapping around my body and her warm breath on my neck. I put the half-drained bottle of water down on the entryway table. Without thinking it through, I carried her up to her bed.

"You're still taking your birth control, right?" I'd have to force myself to stop if for some reason she'd missed a dose.

Libby nodded. She bit her lip, which seemed to be her wordless plea for a deeper connection. *How can I deny her that?* It had only been two days since we first made love, and I had to be easy with her. I was made to be her predator, and I'd defy that role just to be near her. Libby was already undressing herself, but I halted her by grabbing her hands and finishing the job myself. In less than a minute she was completely naked. So frail, weak, but brave all the same. She lay back as if anticipating my next move. I wasn't sure what that move would be, but she was. I undressed myself and lay by her side. My eyes wanted to fixate on every nuance of her body, but she wouldn't have the patience required for that.

"I need you…" Libby panted.

She wasn't the only one in need.

I kissed her and rested on one arm to brace myself. The other arm trailed down her body and cupped her breast, but I wanted to feel her warmth, the very warmth I couldn't easily produce in my own body. Her breath caught as my hand ran down the inner side of her thigh. She seemed so innocent, though neither of us could claim that.

"Breathe."

She did as I said, though her breathing was still forced. I pushed one finger inside of her as she moaned. I moved my finger in and out as her dew amassed, and her body stiffened. I wanted in but resisted. I moved down so that my face was in between her legs. Her thighs quivered as I flicked my tongue at the crest of her opening. Warmth extended from her body to my mouth. She was scalding in comparison. She spread her legs apart more, giving me room to work. I rolled my tongue from the top of her clit, down toward the opening, dipping my tongue inside until her body spasmed. Her climax was raw and beautiful. I pushed my finger back inside her and felt the fluttering of muscles as they spent themselves to exhaustion.

As her orgasm ebbed, I positioned myself over her to claim her again. The look in her eyes reflected the pleasure she'd experienced. Once her breathing normalized, I guided myself inside. I focused on her eyes all while trying to hold off my own climax. This had to endure, but it was a futile venture. She was so hot and inviting. The way I fit inside of her was indescribable, like our bodies had been molded for the other. She pushed her hips up, taking me deeper. I'd held back, afraid to hurt her, but she craved it all. I moaned as my ejaculation escaped, and I buried my head into the fold of her neck. As it ended, I turned my head away from her neck. The strong aroma of her blood was too close to its surface. I didn't need her blood per se, but it was there, and its scent was sweet.

I pulled out of her and lay down by her side. I scooped her into the spoon position and held her there. One reprieve from this encounter was the lack of bleeding. I could breathe without having to hold my breath.

"I think I love you, Liam." Her voice was weak from exertion.

I traced my hand over her hip. My body pressed to her, holding her there. "I have no doubt about you, Libby. I love you too."

"Don't leave me alone tonight. Stay with me." Her voice was feeble as a child's.

"I won't go anywhere."

She was too tired to move, and so I pulled the covers up over us both. She'd get cold if she stayed like this with me behind her, but the covers would keep her warm enough. She fell asleep. I wasn't tired yet, but I lay there until I was. There was no other place that I would rather be, I thought, and then I too drifted off to sleep.

***

Libby

Today I had to be in the office for a make-it-or-break-it meeting. We had a client coming in from a hotel, which could mean big things to our little office. We'd only be responsible for the design of the hotel lobby and dining room, but that would be more than enough work. We'd likely get more attention from this one job alone than in all of our other smaller jobs combined. Lillian would be heading the project, and the other office's part-time interior designers would also be in on this job. It was an all-hands-on-deck situation. I wouldn't have to do much for the hotel design, since I was working on Liam's project. I'd still need to help out though as needed, and could price materials and create design ideas. It would be experience that would be résumé worthy.

Shelby had called me on Tuesday morning to see if I was available, but after I'd said good-bye to Liam that morning, I'd had to be in the office by nine. Once this project was lassoed, which would be by the end of today's meeting, *fingers crossed*, my life would be my own again. Liam had been over the past few evenings. I was too tired on Tuesday and Wednesday, but having him near while I slept was more soothing than I could have guessed.

The meeting began at ten in the morning. Our conference room was packed, and Lillian's entire staff was present, although that was only five total. Water's Edge Suites was an independent hotel that wasn't affiliated to any other hotel branch. Their brand boasted contemporary luxury, and the rooms were supposed to be spa inspired. The hotel sent four executives here for the meeting, which consisted of three men and one older lady. They seemed polite but wore matching guarded expressions. I tensed when the woman executive looked my way—something about her gaze was critical. When I'd first learned of this meeting, I'd assumed that we had the job, but now I wasn't so sure.

Our office had prepared three design ideas. From the look of the executives' faces, I worried that they'd reject all the mockups. When the contract seemed to be lost, Lillian was offered the job. We all kept quiet and let Lillian speak to thank them and to accept their offer. *Thank God...*

The meeting had been surreal, but not in a good way. Lillian pulled me aside, and I thought she would assign me a duty to complete for the new project. But no, she just wanted to tell me that Christian had spoken to Sarah and that things looked promising so far. That news made me happy. At least work shouldn't be as awkward after Christian's advances. I hadn't spoken to Sarah in a few days, but other things were occupying my mind. *Liam...*

I went to my desk after the executives left, and tidied it up. I wasn't here every day, and it always seemed like things got moved around while I was gone. The bright-blue stapler that I'd bought was never on my desk. It was as if it hopped desk to desk. Today it was by the copy machine, in neutral territory. The next item on my agenda was to go out for coffee with Shelby, although I'd need something more substantial too, since it was lunchtime. For once my hunger wasn't gnawing away at me. Maybe Shelby had finally rubbed off on me? Before long I'd need no nutrition at all? *Yeah, right!*

I drove to the coffee shop, which wasn't far from work. I frequented the coffee shop for quick lunches or lattes on the go. Once inside I spotted Shelby sitting at one of the small tables toward the back. Her hair looked so glossy in the fluorescent lighting, which was odd because fluorescent wasn't the most flattering. I was beginning to think that she could wear a garbage bag as a dress and still look glamorous. Had she sold her soul to the devil? That would explain it...

We both ordered at the long counter and waited for our food to arrive back at the table she'd picked out. We hadn't ordered much—Shelby had asked for a black coffee, and I wanted a vanilla chai tea with an orange scone. Shelby's drink wasn't something she'd ever ordered before. Usually she drank coffee with equal parts sugar and cream or hot chocolate, but I'd did my best to behave and not criticize her order. Our drinks and my scone came out moments later. The scone's icing dripped over its sides.

"So how did the meeting go with the hotel people?" Shelby sounded like her normal self, but after her absence on Monday, she was still holding a grudge.

"We got it! I won't really have to do much for the project itself, but it'll be great for the office. I mean, who knows what it will lead to." I couldn't help but be excited—it was excellent news. Professionally, I'd have a secure job for years to come, and that was something I wouldn't take for granted in a small town.

Shelby's smile was familiar. She held the coffee cup between her hands, for warmth I'd assumed. Her coffee was still too hot to drink, with its steam billowing from the mug. "That's great! I'm sure it will turn out perfect."

"Thanks." I would still have to apologize, but things were going so smooth that I didn't want to go there just yet. I wanted to enjoy this time with my friend without the worries that radiated throughout my mind. I wasn't really worried about hurting her feelings, but I wanted to address her eating disorder. It still didn't seem like Danny had even noticed. Was

I the only one who really cared about Shelby's health? The finality of what I needed to do overwhelmed me, but I had no other options now.

I looked into Shelby's eyes, which somehow looked different than what I'd remembered—they twinkled more. "I'm sorry about the toast." I'd start simple and then move into the heavier issues.

"It's okay, Libby. I'm already over it." Shelby didn't like conflict, but I couldn't help it.

"Actually, I'm not. I'm worried about you. I never see you eat anymore, and you're so thin that I wonder if you might have an eating disorder." I reached out to touch her hand, but stopped when I saw her facial expression change into something…neither anger nor denial, but guarded maybe. She wasn't upset?

She laughed as if I'd said something hilarious. "I don't have an eating disorder. I eat plenty."

Something in the way she was looking at me caused my hair to stand on end. "Then why don't I ever see you eat anything anymore?"

"Well, you saw me eat toast, didn't you?"

Sarcastic much?

"Besides that, I haven't seen you eat a thing." I didn't want to give in yet, even though every nerve in my body warned me to drop it.

Shelby then did something that I couldn't understand. She stared deep into my eyes and said, "I'm fine, Libby. You know that I'm fine. There is nothing to worry about." Then she sat back in her chair and sipped at her coffee as if nothing had happened.

I didn't know what to say, but I believed her and decided not to worry anymore. I picked at my scone and sipped on my chai tea. After I'd finished the food, my head cleared, and nothing seemed to bother me at all. She didn't even look as thin now, though she was still plenty skinny.

"We'll have to do this again." She stood to leave and hugged me. I nodded. It had been nice. Shelby's complexion looked radiant, maybe even glowing. Why had I been so hung up on her eating? It all seemed silly now.

Once I was back to work, the haze I'd been under diminished, and I wondered if I'd had a sugar high. My stomach ached, and I instantly regretted the scone, which must have been the culprit. I dashed to the restroom just in time to empty the contents of my stomach. Soured vanilla tea was all I could taste. My shoulder banged into the bathroom stall as I stood and tried to steady myself. My forehead didn't feel hot, but a fever didn't always accompany an illness. *The stomach flu. Great...* I went home early and lay on my sofa because that was all the energy I could muster.

Chapter 5

Plus Sign

Libby

Going to Ocean City wasn't something I'd done in years, other than to visit the bars. The sun beamed down on my face, and it was warm for early April. Trimper's Rides weren't usually open this early in the season, but since there was a car show in town, Trimper's decided to open their gates.

"Come on." Liam motioned for me to get on the antique carousel.

I grabbed his offered hand and stepped up on the ride's platform. I mounted a classic white stallion with purple reins, while Liam rode the ostrich to my left. I laughed at the faces he made as we both went up and down, but not at the same time. It was almost sexual.

The next ride we braved was called the Endeavor—like a Ferris wheel but much faster. Views of the beach, parking lots, vendors, and building tops flew by and seemed fun to watch, at first. The urge to keep watching the scene as it whizzed by compelled me, but soon the initial delight yielded to nausea. I closed my eyes tight, sealing out every beam of light until I could only see a red haze through my eyelids. Liam grabbed my hand and uttered reassurances, but they were lost to the sound of rushing air. The ride lasted minutes longer, and at last...relief.

Motion sickness didn't end our good times though. Not all rides caused that same miserable rush. Maybe this was why I hadn't been to an amusement park since I was a child. Also, I had to rely on my mom to take me, since my dad was long gone by then. When my dad left, my childhood ended.

We hit most every ride that was offered, including the Teacups, Zipper, and Tilt-A-Whirl, and we finished on the roller coaster adequately named Tidal Wave. The stomach flu I'd caught still hadn't completely cleared. My appetite was back for the most part, but then out of nowhere I was throwing up again. The rides had been fun, but now I needed a reprieve to keep the flu at bay.

We ducked into the Dough Roller for pizza—well, Liam had wine.

"That's all you're having?" He was a tall guy. Wine alone wouldn't fill him. Besides, it seemed like I was the only one who ever ate solid food.

"I think the rides took my appetite." He didn't look queasy, but what was there to argue? I'd been ready to vomit on the Endeavor.

"Mine is back and ready to go."

He watched me eat everything but the crust on a small cheese and bacon pizza. My food choices had gone downhill since I'd been with Liam. If I didn't change things soon, the scale would show it. My leggings were stretchy, but they were at their capacity.

***

I lay on my sofa…again. I said prayers in my head for healing, but still the flu had me in its grasp. I was supposed to be working today, but moving off this sofa wasn't an option. I went to the urgent care center days ago because I thought I'd been battling it long enough at that point, but I was assured I'd probably contracted the virus that was still going around. I didn't have strep throat or mononucleosis, so I was released with a bag of generic cough drops, nasal salt water spray, and Zofran for nausea. The physician's assistant said that postnasal drip was what made me nauseated and could've caused vomiting. Never had I had allergies nor needed as much as an eye drop to quell alleged seasonal discomfort.

So I'd just have to tough it out. They told me to return if I had a fever that reached one hundred and three degrees Fahrenheit, or if this persisted over a week, which of course, it had. Liam urged me to go back, but I just couldn't. Something would have to be done today though. I couldn't keep food or liquids down anymore. The only bright spot was that I wouldn't have to worry about dieting since I couldn't keep anything down long enough to absorb its calories or fat. Was this terminal? My ribs ached from all of the heaving I'd done. *I'm so over this.*

"That's it, Libby." Liam's voice was stern. He'd taken care of me for days, but this was the first time in two weeks that I couldn't shake it off and go to work. "We're going somewhere, now!" He wasn't joking.

I looked at him through half-shut eyes and recognized the expression he wore…*fear*. I'd moved into the bathroom to be close to the toilet, and savored the cool floor tiles on my skin. He scooped me off of the floor. I didn't resist or argue, because I was tired of this too.

"Do you think I'm dying?" I didn't think he would admit to anything that horrendous, but what if I was?

"No, Libby, I don't think you're dying." His voice sounded strained, as if the idea of my demise unnerved him.

He put me in my SUV in the passenger's side and buckled me in. I looked terrible, but for once I didn't care. He'd given me a bucket to hold on to. It was a short ride, but I couldn't trust my stomach. When Liam drove in the opposite direction of the urgent care center, it dawned on me that we were hospital bound. So the ride wouldn't be short, and it would take at least thirty minutes to get to Salisbury. I closed my eyes to block out the morning sun and fell asleep.

I woke to the unbuckling of my seat belt and to Liam's arms lifting me out of the SUV. He carried me inside to the emergency department. The weather had warmed up, so I didn't need a jacket anymore, but Liam still wrapped a blanket around me, like I was an infant.

Once inside we were directed to a small cot in the emergency department. The rooms were nicer than I remembered and were actual rooms, not curtain walls, though I saw a section of those on the other side of the ED. We were told that someone would come to collect my insurance and identification information.

I closed my eyes again, wanting to give way to sleep, but an older lady came through the door, pushing a laptop on a tall cart. Liam answered her questions, and he'd given her my insurance card to copy. After she left, a male nurse entered to collect my vital signs and ask about my symptoms. I lay there while Liam detailed my illness to the nurse. Liam told him that I'd been sick for twelve days on and off and that it all started with vomiting and fatigue. In that time the symptoms had only worsened. Liam said that mono and strep were ruled out and that it was assumed I had the flu. I hadn't had the flu vaccine, and it was supposed to be spreading throughout the community.

My blood pressure reading was on the low side of normal. The nurse said a low blood pressure could account for the fatigue. Minutes after the nurse left, the doctor arrived. From what I could tell, the doctor was a kind older woman with powdery white hair. Liam remained by my side while she examined me. He held me up while she listened to my lungs. A scale was brought in the room to weigh me. I'd lost weight since I couldn't keep anything down, and so I'd need fluid-replacement therapy.

I couldn't believe the numbers on the scale, since my pants still fit snug to my waist. I was a slight one hundred and ten pounds. The doctor said that my BMI was too low at 16.7. Apparently a normal BMI was somewhere in between 18.5 and 24. Dr. Curtz wasn't pleased and had me lay back down on the cot. She admitted me to the hospital and would do testing once

I was up on the unit in a private room. She didn't think I was contagious, due to the duration of my symptoms, but I was still put on isolation as a precaution, since vomiting was involved.

Once I was in my room, Liam helped me to change into the horrid hospital gown, and then the phlebotomist came in to take my blood. Liam asked if I wanted him to leave, which of course I didn't. I held his hand with my free hand as the blood was drawn.

Liam looked a little pale as the phlebotomist inverted the tubes to mix them with the additive. After that, the unit nurse and her assistant entered. The assistant took my vital signs again, and the nurse introduced herself as Donna. After her assistant left the room, Donna placed an IV into my left forearm. I didn't realize how disgusting it'd be, but she'd put a white towel under my arm, and blood poured out onto it until she released the tourniquet and clamped the tube to its connector. *Gross...*

I thought that Liam would pass out, but he snapped out of his trance as I started to heave at the sight of blood. Donna placed a basin in my lap and then emptied it for me. She told me that I wasn't allowed to eat or drink anything for the time being and that the IV fluids would help to rehydrate me. She injected something into my IV for nausea, telling me it'd make me drowsy. Since I'd been nothing but drowsy, it didn't matter.

Once Donna left, Liam climbed into bed with me. The bed felt more like a cradle, it was so small, especially with the length of Liam's body sprawled across it. It didn't matter really. I plastered myself against him. I had a bone-deep chill that I couldn't shake. He didn't warm me up, since he was cold like me, but having him near was all that mattered. He'd called Danny to tell him where we were and that the doctor was keeping me here until she knew what was up with me. He'd told Danny not to come, just in case I was contagious, especially since I was now on isolation. Liam looked calm, but there was an anxious air about him, and I wondered what he thought was wrong with me. I lay there motionless as Liam stroked my back.

At around three o'clock, Dr. Curtz knocked on the door as she entered. I was half-asleep but roused when she stood at the foot of my bed. At some point, Liam had moved to the chair.

Dr. Curtz smiled, and her cloud of snowy hair shook as she spoke.

"Most of your tests are back, and you're off of isolation. The blood cultures will take a couple of days, but I don't think they will show us much. There were no traces of any viral or bacterial infections at this point."

Why was she smiling when I had a rare disease? Maybe she was trying to look optimistic before she told me I was a goner?

"What's wrong with her, Doctor?" Liam's voice was husky.

I steadied myself for what was to come.

"Actually, I guess I should tell you both congratulations." Dr. Curtz still wore the same euphoric expression.

"What do you mean?" My tone was harsh, but enough was enough.

"You're expecting." Dr. Curtz shook Liam's trembling hand.

I froze. What could I say? How was this supposed to make me feel, because I was scared. I wasn't planning on this, but I hadn't been as careful as I should've been either. Liam would take care of me if something happened, and so I'd missed my birth control pill a couple of times. I didn't really think much of it at the time. I hate taking pills, and besides, I thought the pill was stronger and would somehow catch up for the pills I'd missed. And I'd never gotten pregnant before when I'd forgotten to take that damn pill.

Liam hadn't spoken. Was he in shock too?

"How far along am I?" I'd only been with Liam a few weeks, but he was the only one I'd been with at all since I'd first met him.

"Oh, it's early. Technically you'd be one-month pregnant according to the blood work, which meant you would have conceived about two weeks ago. Morning sickness this early on is rare, but it happens. We'll get a better due date once we input the date of your last menstrual period into the equation," Dr. Curtz said.

I shook my head, terrified of what Liam was thinking. He still hadn't said a word. "When can I go home?"

"We'll rehydrate you first, and you'll need to be on antinausea medications until your morning sickness ends. So you'll probably be here for a couple of days at the maximum," Dr. Curtz said.

I thanked her and tried to smile.

After she left, Liam crawled back in bed with me, and I lay on his chest. I cried, but I tried not to move. I didn't want him to know how scared his silence had made me. Wasn't he the strong one?

***

Liam

I'd used extra fabric softener on the bed linens to prepare for Libby's arrival. She was brittle, and it was hard to guess how she'd adapt to a new environment even after having previously been in my guest bed at Danny's house. This wasn't the most ideal place for her recuperation, but it was the best option we had. I'd shelter her as much as I could. For now that meant fluffing pillows and adding blankets to the already tidied bed. At least she'll have Shelby too. That would help ground her here. The week had been full of blurry memories, IV lines, blood draws, and trying to find something to feed Libby that wouldn't make her vomit. So far all I'd found was Arby's roast beef sandwiches. Somehow I'd remained by Libby's side for the most part, with the exception of when I'd had to feed.

The hospital brought on a new set of challenges, strange smells, and the scent of sick blood. There was an overwhelming sense of malady that hung in the air. It was inescapable in the hospital's confines. One reprieve was that Libby remained tired from her condition. She was getting IV rehydration and didn't notice when I came and went. I didn't have to explain where I slipped away to or why I wasn't eating. She still didn't know the lie I hid, and the realization that I had to tell her grew every day, like the fetus she carried. After we were given the news, I couldn't think of anything to say, not when I'd hidden something from her that could change everything.

She didn't know the months of illness she would have to endure all because of what I was. Would she really want the child of a monster? Once she learned the truth, she'd need to make a decision whether to stay with me or leave.

I guess on some level I'd known all along that it'd take something dramatic for me to tell her what I was. Maybe I should've been more forthcoming to begin with, but I'd never have predicted any of this. Once the word *vampire* was uttered, she'd leave to protect the baby.

I came home from the hospital early this morning and readied my room at Danny's for her arrival. Even though she'd prefer to go back to the town house, it'd be easier to take care of her at Danny's since my room was on the main level. She'd talked about going back to work as early as next week, but soon she'd realize it wouldn't be possible. Babies bred by a male vampire and a female human wreaked havoc on the mother's body, and her condition wouldn't improve much until the child was born. I packed her a bag from her town house to hold her over on her daily supplies and garments, though she'd soon need maternity clothes. I wanted to make the transition to Danny's house an easy one for her. In a few months I'd have my own house, which we could move into together…if she'd even go for that.

Shelby had been taking over for me when I had to leave the hospital to feed. She was doing this for Libby, I knew, but it felt less overwhelming having her around. I still worried how Shelby had managed herself in the hospital, as nothing was more distracting than the scent of blood. To a new vampire, this has to be torture for Shelby. Danny had also done what he could by ordering more human blood, as I'd need it, especially after being in the hospital. Danny had pushed for me to be transparent with Libby since we'd gotten close, though he had no suggestion on how to do it successfully. Then there was Shelby, who didn't want me to tell Libby anything, so no matter what I did, I'd make someone unhappy.

For now, Shelby waited with Libby for the hospital discharge paperwork.

Danny had been buried in his office all morning long and said that he had a few calls to make. His footfalls clicked on the hardwood flooring, and then he appeared in my doorway.

"I've found a doctor for Libby." His jaw-length hair was wild, and he looked as sleepless as I'd been.

"What?" A doctor for Libby?

"Yeah. I've got a contact through Bio-Nutri-Express. You know, where I order the human blood."

He stared at me like I was an imbecile.

"Okay?"

"That company is run by vampires. They're not new to the challenges we face, obviously, so I called them."

Could I trust a stranger with Libby, much less another vampire? "Continue…"

"There's a physician that they have on staff. He was a doctor before he was changed." Danny looked at me as if to gauge my reaction.

"So he's one of us?" I worried about the blood, Libby's blood. Giving birth would entail a lot of blood.

"Yes, and he's been a vampire for over a hundred years. He's had a lot of exposure with human blood, and several pregnancies like Libby's, with a decent record of successful births."

This could give her a fighting chance. Having someone on our side to bring her through it, that'd be what she needed. "When can we meet him?"

"He'll arrive tomorrow. He's got to fly in from Canada. From what I learned on the phone, her care will be specialized. He'll be here until she gives birth."

I wasn't sure if I really wanted to share this with an unknown doctor, but I didn't have a choice. I'd have to do whatever it took to keep Libby alive and the baby safe. "Thank you." Danny didn't have to do this, and he was more supportive than I could've imagined. "I'm sorry to bring this down on both you and Shelby."

"There's nothing to be sorry for. You and Libby were drawn together. It wasn't just about you. I'm sure you know that already, don't you?"

I did know and had tried to shut her out in the beginning. But then Sam had captured her. After that I couldn't, and didn't, want to keep her away. "I know you're right, but I wish it didn't have to be this way. I know Shelby hates me now, not that I can blame her for that."

"She doesn't hate you, Liam. She doesn't understand. She thought that she could protect her friend from this fate, even though she doesn't regret it for herself. She'll come around." He grabbed my shoulder and embraced me for a second before letting go. I couldn't image how I'd ever repay his generosity. He was the brother I came back for. *Thank God for that.*

Shelby called and said that they would be home within the hour. Libby's clothes were hanging in my closet, and fresh sheets were on the bed. I'd stocked the kitchen with food that I hoped she'd be able to tolerate. I fed one more time to assure myself I was really ready for her.

By four o'clock, Shelby pulled into the driveway, which looked crowded with Danny's truck, Shelby's car, and Libby's SUV. I'd brought Libby's SUV here, not wanting it to sit in front of the town house unattended. I'd thought that I would get a vehicle of some kind too, but with all the vehicles around, I'd wait until I had a place to park it. I went outside to meet the girls, and I lifted Libby out of the seat.

"I've got you, lightweight." She was no heavier than a house cat.

"Yes, you do…" Libby whispered in my ear.

Shelby brought in the few possessions that Libby had at the hospital, along with her newly prescribed prescription medications. I didn't want her taking the medications if she didn't really need them, since I couldn't guess what kind of side effects they'd have, but hoped the doctor would have a safe solution for Libby once he arrived.

Libby leaned into me as I carried her inside. She still seemed too frail and was weak, without much to say. The fatigue she suffered seemed to drain her of all signs of life, which was odd since she normally had a vibrant personality.

After being in the hospital, a bath was in order. Shelby followed us to the bathroom like a mother hen. She helped me undress Libby as the water filled the bathtub. With Shelby in tow, this potentially provocative moment was shattered. Under normal circumstances Libby would object to this degree of babying, but she wasn't in any condition to fight us. How could a hospital discharge someone as ill as Libby still was? Once Libby was completely naked, Shelby gasped at the frail skin and bones of her best friend.

"She looks so malnourished." Shelby wiped a tear from her eyes.

"I know… Did Danny tell you about the doctor that's coming?" It pained me too, but Libby wouldn't see me cry, just in case some part of her understood what was going on.

"What doctor?" Shelby sniffled.

"A doctor that's like us. Apparently he's helped patients like Libby before." I sounded confident but was still uncertain. If Libby remained under the care of human physicians, she wouldn't survive this. Her body wasn't absorbing the nutrients that she needed to maintain a pregnancy, much less her own life. She looked from me to Shelby but didn't ask questions.

"Good. She needs that." The tension that Shelby carried seemed to ease. I hoped that the doctor could help. He had to.

After we bathed Libby, Shelby helped me to dress her and put her in bed. I tried to feed Libby, but she refused to eat anything and muttered that she felt too sick even with the antinausea medication. Tomorrow couldn't come soon enough.

***

I'd been up with Libby all night, watching her restless sleep. She'd vomited twice, and each incident left her listless and covered in a sheen of perspiration.

Shelby knocked and came inside the bedroom. "He's here. Danny's helping him inside. I'll stay with Libby while you speak to him." Shelby pulled a chair closer to the bed and took her friend's hand.

As I walked toward the living room, I pushed my hair back in the hope of looking saner. At present I had to look as crappy as I felt. Danny pushed open the front door while carrying two thermal bags that the doctor must have brought with him. Behind Danny was the doctor. The redheaded doc pulled a large suitcase behind him and had a duffel bag slung over his shoulder. He had a distinct look. His dark-red hair was slicked back in the same style Elvis Presley had combed his hair in his younger days, but on the doctor, it looked less Hollywood and more debonair.

Danny nodded in my direction. "That's my brother, Liam. He's the father."

The doctor's eyes met mine. He shifted his duffel bag and presented his hand to me. "Nice to meet you, Liam. I'm Abraham Shirley. After I'm settled, we'll need to talk. Then I'd like to examine your mate."

I smiled at the word *mate* and thought Libby would scoff at such a term. But then again, she wouldn't know what the term *mate* meant to vampires.

Danny took the doctor to the basement, where he'd converted his secondary office into a guest room. About fifteen minutes later, Abraham returned to the main level. Danny had already disappeared into his main office.

"Shall we have a seat?" Abraham said as he headed toward the living room seating area.

I followed him and felt like I was in his space. His presence was commanding, and for some reason that quality seemed important. He carried himself in a way that made me feel like he was the answer to keeping Libby alive.

"Thank you for coming here."

Abraham sat back but still had perfect posture. "I go where I'm needed."

"I appreciate that. Libby isn't doing well." My stomach knotted at the admission of her status, as if saying it aloud would somehow make it truer.

"I assumed that she isn't doing well. Humans weren't made to carry our babies, even though the fetus itself will be born human."

Abraham spoke scientifically, but it still hurt to hear.

"We didn't mean for this to happen. She was supposed to be on the birth control pill." I looked down at my hands, ashamed of what I'd done to her.

Abraham stiffened and spoke through clenched teeth. "Were you hoping to have her burden relieved?"

My eyes shot back up to look him in the eye. "No! That's not what I meant at all. We both want the child."

Abraham's jaw unclenched, and his voice softened. "I'm sorry to speak so impassioned, but I've been asked to do that procedure before. One thing I don't do is take life. I only help to maintain, when I can."

"She doesn't know what I am…or what any of us are." I didn't know what he'd recommend, but this was something he had to know.

"Hmmmm…" Abraham held his chin. "That will make things more difficult. Once she's lucid, she will have to know."

I took a deep breath and hoped it would calm me down. "Is there any way of breaking the news to her in a way that wouldn't upset her or the baby?"

"Once I have her stabilized, she'll be in no harm of losing the fetus, if that's what you're worried about?"

"Not only that. I don't want her to leave the care that you can provide for her either."

Abraham seemed pleased with my statement. "She won't want to leave my care. It's the only way she will have any relief as long as she's pregnant."

"What is the treatment?" I hoped it wasn't vile.

"First, you'll have to understand that I was a trained human physician. I was changed about one hundred years ago and was already a practicing doctor at the time. I first tried to retain my human job but found it too difficult with all of its temptations, until I had more exposure. So I transitioned into working concierge for other vampires to treat their human companions. I've been at this job long enough that human blood doesn't appeal to me anymore. I've been with Bio-Nutri-Express for about thirty years. I've assisted thirty births with this company and helped to save the mother in eight other maternity cases. Those women received care late in their pregnancies and were lucky to survive it themselves. They were emaciated, dehydrated, and too far along to support their babies." Abraham shifted in the chair before continuing. "For your mate, I'll need to examine her first. I'll monitor her condition and progress to assure that she's on target with her pregnancy. The primary treatment is frequent blood transfusions. So in the first exam, I'll also type her blood and match her to an acceptable donor blood."

"When will she be able to communicate more normally?" It wasn't that she was totally out of it, but she wasn't herself in any capacity.

"From what I've seen, your mate should be communicative as soon she receives her first blood transfusion."

After we finished talking, I showed Abraham to Libby's bed. Her eyes were closed, and her breaths were short and erratic. Abraham carried an old leather doctor's bag, which looked like it was an original from the time he began practicing medicine. He made small talk with Libby as he prepared her arm for the blood draw. Libby didn't respond, but Abraham still told her every move he made, as though she'd asked. This was reassuring.

"How far along is she supposed to be?" Abraham asked as he palpated Libby's abdomen.

"We were told that she was just over a month along."

"Too soon to hear the heartbeat then. I'm going to have to check her uterus manually." He slid on gloves in preparation.

My cheeks burned. Was he was going to violate Libby right in front of my eyes? I had to swallow down my anger because it didn't belong here. Abraham didn't seem to need my assistance, but I helped anyway by removing the blankets and arranging Libby. I didn't want to watch, but at the same time I wouldn't let him at her without me there as her protector. Libby made a pained squeaking sound.

"Her cervix is tender. That's normal." Abraham pulled his hands away and removed his glove.

I settled the blankets back into place around Libby.

"Everything felt normal. I'm not sure if she'll have a single birth or perhaps multiples. The gestational sac felt a little enlarged. That could be from the size of the fetus, or in some cases multiple births. She's thin, but that's expected at this point. She'll begin to gain normal pregnancy weight once she's receiving her transfusions. We'll know by this afternoon what type of blood she can tolerate, at which point we will begin her first transfusion."

I listened to Abraham but was more concerned with the chattering of Libby's teeth. If I could, I'd warm her up myself, but my body would only cool her down even more.

Abraham went down to his room and retrieved a heating blanket he'd brought with him. He tucked the warm blanket over Libby, and her chattering teeth slowed. He set the control to the highest setting, and I hoped this would help her until the blood could be delivered.

A Bio-Nutri-Express laboratory courier arrived after Libby was settled back down. They would call as soon as they'd processed Libby's blood sample.

Abraham went back down to the basement, as there wasn't anything more he could do until it was time to transfuse Libby. He'd also brought his own blood to feed on. From what Danny learned, Abraham only consumed animal blood. Since Abraham lived in Canada, he'd grown accustomed to the diet that the Canadian wilderness offered. So as long as Abraham stayed here, Bio-Nutri-Express would deliver him fresh moose blood, bear blood, caribou blood, and his favorite, Dall sheep blood.

***

Libby

Was I dreaming? My skin tingled like I was lying by a roaring fire. I didn't think I'd ever warm up again.

"Well hello," said a strange male voice.

I opened my eyes and focused on a handsome red-haired man. He sat by my bed, rather, Liam's bed, as if we'd met before. He was angular with high cheekbones, and his hair was glossy and combed away from his face. He was as attractive as Liam, though there wasn't any physical similarities.

"Who are you?"

"Forgive me. I'm your doctor. You can call me Abraham." His voice was clear and soothing, like a doctor's voice should sound.

"I have a doctor? Here, I mean?" I looked around the room and noticed what looked like a bag of blood hanging on an IV pole. The red-filled plastic tubing led right to my blanket-covered arm. There wasn't a fire like I'd imagined, but I was wrapped up in an electric blanket. The thought of the blood dripping into my vein made me heave. The sight of blood usually didn't bother me, but now, everything bothered me.

"Whoa now." Abraham placed a basin in my lap and rubbed my back. His touch was familiar in a way I didn't understand.

Nothing came up, and I lay back as sweat rose across my forehead. I didn't like seeing blood like that. It looked sinister.

Abraham set the basin back on the side table. "To answer your question, yes, you do have a doctor here. You'll be getting blood transfusions throughout your pregnancy. It's vital for the health of you and your child."

I spoke through dry lips. "The sight of the blood hanging like that is making me nauseated." I kept my eyes closed because I'd be drawn to the bag of blood.

"Well, Libby, I might have a solution for that."

I opened my eyes to see what he was up to. He dug into what looked like an old doctor's bag and pulled out tubing. He held up what he'd found. "This is colored tubing. You won't be able to see through it." He unwrapped the blue tubing and stretched it out. "If you wouldn't mind, close your eyes for this part. I don't want you to see the old tubing as it's removed, or you may feel sick again."

I did as he'd asked and kept my eyes closed. He took my wrist, and his icy hand extended my arm to get access to the hub of the IV. Within a minute, he'd finished.

"Okay, you can open your eyes now."

I opened my eyes, and there was now blue tubing running to my arm. My eyes followed it up toward the blood bag that he'd covered with a brown paper bag. I breathed out. "Thank you. That's much more tolerable."

"I aim to please." He winked at me.

"How long will I be bedridden?" I was better than I had been and wanted to go back to work as soon as I could. As well as I felt, I couldn't imagine I'd be here long.

His expression changed. He looked serious, as if he didn't want to answer my question. "Well, you won't be bedridden per se, but you will need to stay at least within the parameters of this house for the most part."

I gasped as tears welled up and spilled onto my cheeks. "What do you mean? I can't leave this house?"

"What you don't understand is how delicate your condition is. You'll need the blood to keep you and your baby alive. This is why you need to remain close by. The transfusions will be frequent, or you will without a doubt lose your baby, and maybe even perish yourself."

"Liam!" I screamed. "Liam!" After what felt like a long time, but was probably only thirty seconds, he came through the door, followed by Danny.

Abraham grabbed my shoulder. "Take slow, deep breaths. You're panicking."

I tried to tune him out and moved my shoulder so that his hand fell away.

"I've got her," Liam said as he sat behind me on the bed and pulled my back against his solid chest.

I cried and turned my head to bury myself into Liam. "I don't understand," I said in a whisper to

Liam. "This is not normal. Pregnant women don't get constant blood transfusions, nor are they on house arrest."

"No, Libby, of course you're right. But…" Liam hesitated as if trying to figure out how to tell me something awful. "Libby, you're not pregnant in the traditional sense."

Danny came closer to the bed, and then Shelby came inside the room too. Whatever was happening wasn't good. It was obvious that bad news was coming. Was I even pregnant? Or maybe the child was so deformed that extraordinary measures would be the only chance of its survival?

"What do you mean?" I looked up at Liam and then around the room. Everyone looked scared. Whatever it was, it was bad.

"It all began with me," Danny said. Shelby wove her fingers through his, and she looked up at him. "Two hundred years ago, something happened that changed my existence. I didn't know it at the time, but because of me, we've all been cursed." Danny looked at Shelby and then to Liam.

Two hundred years ago? Had they all lost their minds? "Danny, what the hell are you talking about?"

Danny continued on without preamble. "After I was turned, Liam came looking for me. I thought that I could protect him by leaving, but then he fell into the same fate as me. He then changed his wife, Ciara, though we didn't all reunite until recently."

"This makes no sense!" I looked at Abraham. He sat there listening as if this all was logical.

"Unfortunately for Shelby, we'd grown close. The one who created me kidnapped Shelby and tortured her. Shelby was nearly dead when we found her, and the only option to save her life was to change her too."

Change? Change into what? "I have no idea what you're even talking about."

"Libby, we're not human. None of us are," Danny said.

Liam held me close, and I shivered. Both from the coolness of his body and from the declaration that none of them were human. "If not human, then what?" The key to it all was the only thing they apparently didn't want to tell me.

"When one of our kind impregnates a human, then that pregnancy is deadly to the human if they are not given the appropriate treatments. A human physician wouldn't understand how to best care for you, and you would die. Your baby will be born human of course, but the way our DNA merges with your DNA is toxic to the mother," Abraham said as if his scientific words would make sense of this mess.

"Aliens?" I asked. If I sounded crazy, then I would sound just like everyone else here. Liam still held me. Maybe he was afraid that I'd rip out the IV and run?

Liam bent forward and whispered in my ear. "Please don't be scared of me."

"Maybe I wouldn't be if you were honest with me. What are you?" My voice shook.

He swallowed. "Vampire," Liam said in a hushed tone.

That was it, all I could take. The craziness, the lies. I had to get away. Adrenaline kicked in, and I pushed off Liam and bolted toward the door. I'd forgotten about the IV pumping blood into my arm. I heard the tape rip before I felt the pain. The IV pulled out of my arm, and a spray of blood shot into the air. I looked down to see a stream of blood run down my arm in ribbons. The adrenaline was no match for my newly acquired aversion to blood, and I planted facedown onto the hardwood floor. My sight betrayed me, and ringing surged in my ears.

When I came to, Liam stood by the bed holding my other hand. Abraham had reinserted an IV and had already restarted the transfusion. Danny stood by the door, looking like a bouncer in a night club. I wouldn't be able to run out again while he was there on guard. Shelby had left the room.

"Are you okay?" Liam asked. His eyes looked lost.

I didn't want to answer. Not after such a betrayal. "Where's Shelby?"

"Too much blood. It's a temptation for her. She's a new vampire," Danny said.

I rolled my eyes. "So we're still on that, are we?" Their lie had nearly killed me.

"It's the truth, Libby. I'm sorry that it's like this, but that is my reality," Liam said.

"Prove it," I muttered. Not that I wanted proof because it'd be gross, but it was the only way. These lies had to end.

Liam's eyes looked pained. He turned to look back at Danny, who nodded once. "Are you sure about this?" Liam asked.

"You have to do it if you want me to believe this insanity."

Liam leaned into me as if he was going to kiss my neck. He stalled but then moved so that his lips grazed over my jugular. His teeth sank into me like I was an apple. I gurgled as nausea churned in my stomach. The pain wasn't so bad, and then even that was replaced by more pleasurable sensations. I moaned and cut it off, as I realized that we weren't alone. He pulled away, and I saw my blood on his mouth. He wiped the blood away, but that was enough. I lay back as my ears hummed again. I didn't pass out all the way this time, but the truth of it all stung. The lies were all true.

My boyfriend was a vampire…

Chapter 6

Growing Belly

Libby

"How are you feeling today?" Abraham asked as he knocked once and entered the bedroom. During the past month I'd gotten comfortable around him. Once I was over the shock of the word…*vampire*…life here made more sense. Thank God no one ate around me, but to think I thought Shelby suffered from an eating disorder.

"Okay, I guess." I was ten weeks pregnant today and was so much better than I'd been at our first meeting.

Abraham carried a bag of blood to hang. He tried to keep it covered as much as possible, but I'd become used to the routine. A bag a day kept my nausea away.

Abraham bent over me and connected the IV's catheter to the tubing. My arms were covered with bruises from the IVs, though Abraham changed the IV site every four days so that I wouldn't get an infection.

"You're doing very well. Would you mind if I examined you this morning?"

"Go ahead." I pushed the blanket from my lap. Being housebound bored me to tears…I literally cried sometimes. Was I even human anymore? My skin had blanched since I couldn't go to the tanning bed. I didn't overdo the tanning, browning just enough to look healthy and alive. It didn't seem possible to be alive in this house, not since everyone else was undead. The last time I remembered being outside, the air still held a slight chill, but now I assumed it was warmer. I could go out on the front porch or back deck if I wanted to, but what was the point?

Abraham listened to my lungs, checked my pulses, looked into my eyes with a flashlight, and then had me lay back on the bed. I pulled my shirt up to my ribs, as he'd need access to my belly.

He smiled. "You're starting to show." He only saw my belly once a week, but the other routine things he did daily.

"What?" I looked down, embarrassed. I held myself up on my elbows as I watched him examine my slightly rounded belly. It wasn't sizable, but there was a roundness forming under my navel. I jumped as his cool hands moved over what he called the fundus.

"Sorry." His hands were usually cool.

"I should be used to it by now." I couldn't remember when he first started treating me, but that was when I was malnourished by the pregnancy and mentally drained. Now things had changed, and I didn't feel sick anymore. In addition to my daily infusion of blood, I ate whole foods. I couldn't tolerate anything fried or unnatural. I still wanted French fries, but getting sick again wasn't worth the momentary joy a French fry could bring.

"It's hard getting used to us, I know." Abraham's face looked pained, but his tone remained neutral.

He was right about that. The notion was sometimes more than I thought I could handle, but I didn't want to offend him. Not after the care and concern he'd shown so far.

Since Liam had bit me to prove what he was, things were different…strained. What we created together continued to grow inside of me, but we'd forged distance in our relationship. It wasn't fair to either of us. At the same time, I could hardly fight how much I longed for him to bite me again. It was reckless and stupid, but it still nagged at me. Maybe I was deranged? I replayed the thrill his bite had caused in my mind on a daily basis, and fought to push those fantasies down. *He wouldn't understand…* It didn't even seem logical to me.

As Abraham finished with his exam, he pulled my shirt down to cover my belly.

"Libby…" Abraham hesitated but then continued. "Is there something wrong that I can help you with? You've been quieter than usual."

Telling Abraham wasn't something that I'd planned on, but I couldn't tell Liam. I looked down, not wanting to feel the burn of his sparkling blue eyes. "I've been having this craving for some time." My voice was a hushed whisper. This must be how it feels to admit sin in a confessional.

"What kind of craving? I'm sure I can relate."

I laughed like a mental patient. Of course he'd know about cravings. I was sure they all felt the craving for blood, at the very least. "Remember when Liam bit me?" As if he could forget.

"Yes, I was there."

"I want to be bitten again and feel like I need it to survive." I picked at my fingernails and bit my lip. I couldn't meet his eyes to see the judgment that had to be there. I waited for him to speak, but he was silent. I looked up to meet his cyan gaze.

"It's actually a common reaction to the bite itself. Usually you'd have to be bitten more than once though to feel its addictive pull." He paced around the room but then stopped before speaking. "Are you sure that this was your first bite?"

I stared at him, astonished by his question. I had no memory of being bitten before. "Wouldn't I know if I'd been bitten previously?"

"Well, you may not have remembered. We have the ability of being very hypnotic when necessity dictates."

"So you think that someone bit me?" I tried to sort it out in my head. I'd been distant with Liam since I'd found out what he was, and part of that was because I craved something I thought was forbidden. Now I wondered if my cravings were even in my own control.

"It would make more sense if someone did indeed bite you."

I could talk to Abraham candidly, without worrying how he'd react. He cared for me as his patient and was keeping me alive. We'd all put trust in him, and I liked him. "Then what do I do? I mean, to get rid of the cravings?"

"Well, sometimes you have to replace one vice with another." Abraham gave me a look that made me think I should know what he was talking about.

"Like?" Impatience flowed into my tone.

"Well, is there anything else you find particularly craveable?" Abraham looked uncomfortable.

"Do you mean, like sex?" My cheeks burned. Some things were hard to voice, and I didn't want to put images into Abraham's head. The lines blurred enough as it was in our doctor/patient relationship. Trust and intimacy were themselves a fine line.

"Well, yes, that would probably do, but anything really that you desire would work just as well." His face flushed to match my own. "Maybe you should figure out if you were bitten first. At least that would give you some peace of mind."

I nodded. "Can I have…sex? I mean, is it safe?"

His cheeks were now as red as his hair. "Yes, intercourse is both safe and natural." He swallowed. "Since everything looks good here, I'm going to head downstairs for a bit. I'll be back to unhook you when the transfusion is finished," Abraham said and left with a flourish.

I called Liam's name. In the daytime he was either working in the living room on his laptop, or he was over to the building site. Footsteps clicked in my direction.

"Are you okay?" Liam asked as he entered. I hadn't called on him much and realized I'd startled him.

"Well, I have something to ask you." I patted a spot on the bed next to me. He obeyed. He looked on edge. His hazel eyes caught my attention with their superhuman beauty.

"What is it, love?"

"There's a reason that I've acted distant from you lately." Why did I think it'd be easier to verbalize this after talking it over with Abraham?

He raised his brow. "Because I'm a vampire, you mean?"

He thought he scared me, but that hadn't been it at all. Disbelief, yes. Fear, no. "I need to know how many times you've bitten me before." Whatever he thought I was going to say, that wasn't it. His eyes searched mine, as if looking for the reason behind my question.

"Why does that matter?"

"It matters because of the feelings I'm having. Since the time you bit me to prove yourself, I've wanted more of it. I know that I shouldn't, but I do." I raised my hand when I saw he was about to speak. I needed to get it all out at once before I lost my nerve. "I asked Abraham about it, and he said that people don't usually crave to be bitten unless it'd happened on more than one occasion."

Liam looked both angry and torn. "I've bitten you twice," he muttered.

"When? I don't remember." Knowing was more important than anger at this point.

"The time that you first came to see Shelby. She nearly attacked you. She wasn't in control of herself then."

"So why did you bite me then?" I couldn't remember much about that visit, other than the fatigue I'd felt afterward. I'd thought I was getting sick, I'd been so tired.

"To help to calm you. I didn't want you to remember any of it, or you would have known then that Shelby was different, that we all were different." Liam grimaced. "I probably could have made you forget on my own, but the bite really wiped your memory clean."

His admission stung. "Do you trust me now?"

"I love you now, Libby, and more than trust you. I didn't want to expose you to this world. I wanted to protect you from it."

"What happens after this baby is born? I mean, how will that work? I don't want to be old, while you remain young." I'd been thinking this over for a while now, or at least as long as I'd known and accepted the truth.

"You'd regret it and then resent me for changing you into a monster," Liam said, as if he'd thought it over many times before. Of course he'd considered it…that was what he'd done to his widow, Ciara. It still bothered me on some level how long he'd been married before, but that was one of those things I couldn't change no matter what I did. All that really mattered was our future.

"How's it done?" I wouldn't let him derail me. As much as I craved to be bitten again, I also wanted a life with Liam. Not one where he dictated the rules. I needed equality. I didn't care what it'd cost me.

"It can't be done while you're pregnant. You'd lose our child." His voice cracked as he spoke.

"Then when?" He hadn't answered my question, and I hoped there wasn't a loophole to prevent me from causing the change within myself. I had to be like him.

"We shouldn't be discussing this, Libby. This isn't something you'll want."

"That's where you're wrong, Liam. If we're going to be something, then we have to at least be the same species!" I didn't mean to yell, but I had to be heard.

"Our child will be human though!"

"I can't live this way with you and not be able to endure like you." Constriction gripped my chest, and tears betrayed me.

Liam pulled me close and wiped my tears on his sleeve. "Please just think about it. You've got thirty weeks to change your mind. A lot can happen in thirty weeks."

I sniffled and buried my head into his chest. I didn't want to rush into anything, but I'd be damned before I would be the only one who was going to age in this relationship! No miracle face cream or supplement could keep me from growing older. That reality wouldn't go away on its own. Now, it'd take thirty weeks to convince him of that. The same temptation nagged at me again, which meant for now I'd table the problem that couldn't be addressed until I was no longer pregnant. "Abraham also said that I'd need to have sex…"

Liam lifted my chin and smiled. "As long as it's only with me."

***

Today I'd breathe fresh air that wasn't limited to the outer perimeter of Danny's house. The excursion wouldn't be major, but it was now safe enough for me to enter the construction site. As much as I didn't like sitting around, I'd forced myself out on the deck each day for at least an hour for the last week, though I'd napped for most of the time. The diffused lighting triggered drowsiness, and like a basset hound blocking a house's entrance with its body, I slept without shame.

Abraham had already begun my transfusion so that I'd have a little more freedom today. Once the blood had transfused, then I'd have my first ultrasound. His company delivered the bulky machine last night. It was too soon to identify the baby's gender, but getting to see its outline would still be enough.

My clothes didn't fit anymore, and I lived in Liam's oversized shirts and wore elastic-waist capris underneath until the new clothes from Motherhood Maternity arrived in the mail.

"Help me to the bathroom?" I didn't like pushing the IV pole around while blood infused, and my balance was wobblier than it'd been prior to pregnancy.

"You can't yet. Don't you remember Abraham telling you that you would need a full bladder for the ultrasound?"

Liam was right, but I had to go so bad. Maybe I could pee a little…no, I wouldn't stop once I began.

"Crap." I'd downed two glasses of organic milk along with cereal this morning. At least the transfusion was almost over, and then Abraham would be coming to perform the ultrasound.

"I can't wait until you see the cabinets. They're just as nice as you said they'd be."

Of course they were nice. They were premium solid-wood custom cabinets. Even though I couldn't go into work, I still managed to design Liam's house, or was it our house? I was on an extended medical leave from work for what was assumed to be a high-risk pregnancy. I was high risk, no doubt. Lillian visited me once and seemed surprised by my pregnancy, but not as surprised as I'd been.

"Are we ready?" Abraham asked as he walked into the bedroom.

"Her bladder is about to pop," Liam added with a laugh under his breath.

"Okay, we'll get to it then." Abraham turned off the IV pump and disconnected the tubing from my IV. He wrapped the IV's hub in a gauze wrap so that it wouldn't snag on anything while I was out of the house. Abraham pulled the ultrasound machine over to the bedside and waited for me to raise my shirt. He tucked a hand towel into my leggings to prevent the gel from getting on my clothes.

"Ahhhh!" I squeaked as Abraham squirted the cold ultrasound gel onto my belly.

Liam squeezed my hand. Both guys were getting their laughs on my behalf.

Abraham slid the probe of the ultrasound machine over my lower abdomen, and strange black, white, and gray shapes shifted on the screen. "So far it's looking alien." Where was my baby?

"Let it focus." Abraham moved the probe around until it was angled far below my navel.

Once the shape of the head formed, the rest came together. It was an actual human baby, no doubt about it. "Is it okay?"

Abraham moved the probe to the left, which revealed something that I couldn't understand. There seemed to be a fine line on the screen, but then there was another head and body. My throat was dry as realization struck. "Two babies?" How could I manage two?

I turned to Liam, who stared at the screen in what looked like delight.

"So, it looks like I was right with my twin prediction!" Abraham beamed. He continued to measure various things on the screen and said they both had strong heartbeats. He pointed to their hearts. A pulsating cavity cycled in each chest.

After the sonogram, I went to the bathroom. The probe had been torture.

Liam and I walked over to the almost completed house. He smiled like he'd won the lottery, not that he needed the money… No one was working on the house today, and all that needed to be finished were minor fixes inside, as well as the landscaping. The ground around the house was smooth from the leveling work, but those areas were barren, without any kind of foliage. The inspector would be here next week or the following week at the latest, which would then allow us to move in if everything passed inspection. I stomped my feet on the porch, not wanting to track mud inside.

Liam unlocked the glass storm door, and I followed in after him.

"I didn't know it was already set up."

Minor details were missing, like grate covers not being screwed in, but pictures hung on the walls, throw rugs lay in place, and new furniture decorated the rooms. I walked over to the sofa and ran my fingers across the pale buttery leather. I'd used male elements to make the house look like something Liam would live in, but feminine touches to balance out the strong masculine feel. Hot-pink, lime, and turquoise throw pillows rested on the sofa and chairs. Liam took my hand and pulled me into the master bedroom. Danny had made the furniture for this room, and the mahogany bed turned out better than I'd hoped. I ordered the custom mattress that rested on the frame. It had to be made longer to accommodate Liam's height. Sheets and a quilt topped the new mattress. The quilt was a western-style, of all things, but was a compromise of bold colors for me but still sane enough for Liam. Light filtered in through the windows and made the space feel airy and perfect.

Liam looked at me in a way that I'd missed. I bit my lower lip, hoping he wouldn't be too scared to touch me. He'd been cautious since I'd become pregnant. Maybe seeing our healthy babies had somehow eased his mind? Liam locked the bedroom door, though it was doubtful that anyone would disturb us here. I moved my arms up as he pulled the shirt over my head. My body was changing so rapidly that I was nervous I'd mess up my only shot with Liam while I was pregnant. If this first attempt went badly, then I'd likely have a dry spell until after the babies were born.

Once we were both undressed, Liam scooped me up and laid me down with my back against the pillows. He seemed to have a hard time looking away from my swollen breasts, which looked like someone else's. My nipples were larger, and the areolas had darkened to a deeper pink. He tried to caress them, but I yelped in pain. *They hurt.*

His hand went to my open legs and found my clit. He was more delicate than he'd ever been, but he was also persistent on pleasuring me.

My desire for him hadn't been a secret. I opened my legs farther, wanting to give him full access. I wasn't sure how long I lay there moaning, but the ripple of involuntary muscle spasms moved through me, and I screamed. "Oh, Liam!" He didn't stop until my breathing slowed. I didn't know what his plan was, but then he helped me to straddle him.

"You'll have to be on top as long as you're pregnant," he said huskily.

He guided me so that my body sank onto his erection. *It'd been too long since I'd had this.* His face turned red as I moved on up and down on him until I felt his release. It didn't take long. He held me in place, his hands resting on each of my hips. I didn't want it to end…

"You have no idea how beautiful you are right now, do you?"

"Distorted, you mean?" From where I sat atop him, my view was of overly abundant breasts and a rounded belly. Not Victoria's Secret–model material, for sure.

His hands moved over my belly, and he held them there. "No, you're absolutely beautiful. Thank you for carrying my children."

I put my hands over his hands. "Our children." This wasn't a one-sided venture.

After we dressed, Liam made the bed so that it was wrinkle-free. We went back to Danny's house so that I could fix my hair and makeup. Liam promised to take me on a drive, and he owed me one Arby's roast beef sandwich, but no French fries. One thing was for certain at this point—sex had eased my craving to be bitten, though that had already begun to weaken. I still considered Liam's plea for me to remain human, but I had a mind of my own. *Besides, I'm not like Ciara…*

***

Sticky humidity suffocated me as I sat on the porch with the laptop resting on my legs. Fresh air wasn't worth the sweat that clung to my every crease. At fourteen weeks pregnant, I already looked like someone in her fifth month. We were forced to share our twins' news at eleven and one-half weeks with Shelby and Danny—there was just no denying it. My pregnancy had to be hard enough as it was on Shelby, without causing her the envy of my two-for-one deal. I closed the laptop and walked inside. I stood over the air vent to cool my feet. Today was moving day…finally. Danny and Liam transported everything over, including our clothes and toiletries. It'd be weird living somewhere else now, even if it was within walking distance. Abraham would also come with us and would stay until after I'd delivered and had recovered.

Since it was as hot as hell outside, I wore a spaghetti-strap sundress. I couldn't bear the heat anymore, but Abraham assured me that was normal. The babies warmed me like a furnace. My fingers and ankles were swollen, which meant I had to keep my feet up as much as possible…not that it made that much of a difference. When it finally cooled again, I'd have my babies, and Shelby would be married. I'd found a dress for the wedding that was still technically a maternity dress, but something had to be ordered, and I didn't know what I'd be able to fit into after childbirth.

I stretched out on the sofa in the living room and turned on the television. Liam would be over just as soon as the house was all settled, and then he would help me to my new home. Abraham was charged with the task of setting up his medical supplies in the new house, and he'd have to settle himself into our guest room. Shelby was given the duty to babysit me. Apparently I needed constant observation.

"What can I get you for lunch?" Shelby asked. She'd followed me around all morning like I was a toddler on the prowl.

It still felt odd having vampires prepare food for me when their own diet was so singular. Shelby hadn't forgotten what it meant to have a food craving, but she couldn't grasp the degree of my need for food now. Long gone was my nausea and vomiting. Now I was addicted to salty cheeses and organic chocolate without any sense of portion control. Since it was so hot today, I wanted something cooling. "How about a peanut butter and jelly sandwich, with chocolate pretzel bark for dessert?"

"Okay, but wouldn't you rather have a salad with grilled chicken in a light dressing?"

"Definitely not!"

Five minutes later she brought me a plate with my sandwich, two celery logs with peanut butter and raisins, a small dish of chocolate pretzel bark, and a glass of milk.

"Thanks." I took the plate from her hand. Shelby set the milk, the tolerable celery concoction, and dessert down on the coffee table. I took a bite and savored the simple flavors of the sandwich. I wouldn't eat like this for much longer, as it appeared that I wouldn't be eating at all once I was a vampire. Either way, my taste buds had to take in all they could while there was still time. I ate with the intention of enjoying every bite.

"Could you get me a couple of Tums?" Pregnancy gave me scorching heartburn that came every time I had a meal, no matter what it was.

Shelby dropped two Tums into my palm. She sat down beside me and placed her hands on my belly. "How does it feel?" Her eyes were bright. It wasn't the first time she'd asked this, but since my symptoms changed so much, I always had a new answer.

It was bittersweet sharing this with her. Before Danny, she'd gotten pregnant and lost that baby. Now she'd never know what it felt like to carry life within her own body. "Strange. Like my body isn't my own anymore."

"What about when they move?"

I moved her hand so that it was over a spot that had the most activity. From here on out, the babies movements would only increase, though they already took up so much space as it was. Something shifted under Shelby's hand.

"That's incredible." She smiled.

Shelby pulled her hands away and looked satisfied. This was why I didn't like to complain in front of her...she'd never have this.

"How does it feel to be you?"

"You mean to be a vampire?" Shelby seemed a little surprised, but she had adjusted so well that I guessed it was now second nature to her.

I rolled my eyes at her. "Well, yeah."

"Strange in its own sense, I guess." Shelby sat back and crossed her legs on the sofa. She was dressed in weather-appropriate shorts and a tank top, not that the weather affected her.

"Can you elaborate?"

"Things are just effortless now. Getting myself ready doesn't take much time, and it's not like I need to put on makeup anymore. Nothing ever hurts... I don't know." She twirled her finger around a strand of hair. "It's like I've always been this way."

"Do you regret it? I mean, if you weren't dying at the time, would you still want to be a vampire?"

She stiffened. "You don't want this, Lib. You might think you do, but think of your babies. They'll still be human. You'll need to give your kids a normal life." Once again she thought she had all of the answers.

"So you'd just let Danny go and be with him as a human only?"

"I never wanted this for you, Libby, and that's not because I don't want you around. I do, but I'm thinking long term. I don't know what it means to be immortal. I haven't lived long enough to know how that would feel. I imagine that it'll be difficult though."

"Then I guess we're at an impasse." I looked away. How could she have forgotten so quickly how it felt to be in this position? Sure, our circumstances were different, but not our motivations.

In a softer voice she said. "Libby, I will support you no matter what you choose. I know that it's not my decision. I just hope that you consider all of the scenarios you'll have to face. It's not an easy life, but I'm happy. Danny will always be enough for me."

I turned back to look at Shelby and reminded myself that she was my best friend. Her points were valid, but she was living the life I wanted... "I'm sorry to put you on the spot like that." Arguing with her would get me nowhere, and besides, Liam would be the one to change me. *Fingers crossed.*

"I just want you to consider everything in this decision. If you choose this, there's no going back..."

Low blow. As if I'd leave Liam...

She'd put her hand back down on my belly like a magnet to a refrigerator. Was she jealous of me, or was it the lives I carried? "Thank you, Shelby. That's all I needed to know." I couldn't expect her approval. She'd have to adapt to the idea after I was changed.

In the early evening, Liam and I moved into our house. He carried me over the threshold as if we were newlyweds. I worried about the quiet, but we still had Abraham in tow. There'd never be a time when the house was ours alone, and that was a good thing. *I think.*

***

I'd finally hit the official midway mark of pregnancy, but since I was carrying twins, the finish line could come sooner than expected. I needed to hold out until thirty-seven weeks, which was when Abraham said I'd be full term for multiples. My skin was a line-covered map of stretchmarks, and that was with the nightly application of Palmer's stretch-mark oil. *As if I would get through this pregnancy unscathed.* My mirror had confirmed my fate. There was no going back to the girl I once was…

I sat down and put my feet up to get my circulation going again. My ankles were tight with swelling, pins and needles prickling from my knees to toes.

"He's on his way," Liam said as he popped his head into our bedroom. Abraham would be doing my twenty-week ultrasound today and, hopefully, would be able to identify the babies' genders. I'd invited both Shelby and Danny over to view the ultrasound, as this was something I could share with Shelby. It would be a little weird having Danny here too, but Shelby might need him.

Once Abraham set up the ultrasound machine, I lay on the bed, with Liam sitting on one side, holding my hand, and Shelby on the other side, with her eyes glued to the screen. Danny stood by the door and gave us space.

Abraham squeezed an ample amount of gel on my belly—it would take a lot of gel to cover the mass of my expanded bump. The first baby on the screen was labeled twin A. Even though their presence had been made and were evident in my body, it was a relief to see the purposeful twitches of feet and hands. A perfectionist, Abraham checked and rechecked his digital measurements.

"So am I to tell you the gender of these babies?" Abraham smiled. He'd known all along that I had to know.

"You know I want to know." My voice was louder than it needed to be, but I still possessed a little bit of restraint.

"You better let us know before she self-destructs," Liam said with a laugh.

He looked as excited as I felt, and I wondered how he kept his voice so calm.

Danny edged closer to the screen.

Shelby grabbed my hand in a tighter hold, her face neutral, but her grasp was almost unbearable.

"Twin A is a boy!" Abraham said. His voice was more animated than ever, but that could've been because of the general health of the babies, since I was his first twin pregnancy, or his guinea pig, as he sometimes called me.

Abraham moved the probe over to the other side of my belly to find twin B. In all of the excitement of having twins, I hadn't really cared what their genders were. I hadn't planned on becoming a mother, so the preference for one gender over another was a new concept. As Abraham examined twin B and did the measurements to assure his or her health, I tried to guess if the babies would both be male or if I'd have one of each. I didn't know if Liam had a preference either, but like me, he didn't think he'd ever father a child. From what Abraham had told me, the babies shared a placenta but were in their own membranes. So we didn't know if the babies would be identical or fraternal. So did that mean they'd both be boys? I should have listened better when Abraham explained this the first time…

Danny and Shelby and Liam talked casually as Abraham finished up his measurements on twin B.

Most of the conversation was geared to guessing the sex.

"Are we ready now to hear what twin B is?" Abraham asked.

"Yes!"

"Yes," Liam said only seconds after me.

"Well, it's another boy! I believe that they will be identical, though I'll have a colleague verify that." Abraham dried off my belly with a towel.

Liam turned toward me and kissed my lips, cheeks, and forehead. His kisses were short and sweet.

After the ultrasound, Shelby kissed my cheek and went to Danny. Hand in hand, they left. Abraham usually kept a low profile, but he wanted to talk about the details of delivery. The more I learned, the less it should scare me...*right?* How could those sizable babies that I'd just seen on the screen pass through my orifice? Sweat prickled on my forehead. *I can't do this.*

Liam took my hand and pulled me upright. The discussion would take place in the dining room, a more neutral area. The bedroom fostered the images of transfusions and examinations. The dining room was still untainted. I sat down by Liam but couldn't get too close to the table because my bump blocked my attempts.

Abraham cleared his throat. "I think that now is a good time to discuss your delivery." His blue eyes met mine.

"Okay... What did you have in mind?" *Just listen. Don't overthink this.*

Liam watched Abraham with what looked like interest, or was it fear?

"I don't know what your expectations were for the delivery, and I hoped to help you both form a delivery plan." Abraham turned to Liam. "And you, Liam, what level of involvement did you hope to participate in?"

Liam looked guarded. "I want to be there for, Libby, but I'd prefer not to be hands on."

Abraham turned his focus back on me. "I'm sorry to tell you this, but I think a vaginal birth is out of the question for you." Abraham sounded bereaved.

"No, it's okay. The thought of a natural birth turns my stomach." A cesarean birth wasn't much better, but still not as bad as a vaginal birth. At least I couldn't visualize the process of a cesarean. That was a little comforting.

"Why?" Liam asked.

"A cesarean delivery would pose less possible complications. That way we could monitor Libby's progress more thoroughly and retrieve the babies in a controlled environment," Abraham said.

Retrieve? I didn't like how that sounded.

"Would there be a surgical team?" Liam asked.

It was obvious who the responsible one was between the two of us. I wondered if I could leave while they hashed it out, but of course, I couldn't.

"Yes, there's a concierge team that would be assembled. On that team would be an anesthesiologist, a nurse, a general physician, two respiratory therapists, and two pediatricians along with their nurses," Abraham said as he scribbled out the list of labor-day participants on a yellow pad of paper.

"Will the entire team be like us?" Liam asked. That caught my attention—that would be interesting.

"Well, mostly. The pediatricians and their nurses are human, but they'll have no direct interaction with Libby. They would be in the dark about our situation, but that won't impact the care that the babies will receive," Abraham said.

"Well, as long as Libby and the boys are safe, that's all that matters." Liam rubbed his chin.

"I'll do all I can to assure it's so." Abraham eyed each of us, but it'd all been decided.

My delivery was set for mid-November. Abraham didn't want me to go too close to my due date, but at the same time he wanted to assure the babies development would be far enough along so that they would be viable. Apparently Caucasian males were the most fragile of all babies to deliver. Neither Liam nor I could argue with that logic.

The first few weeks in the house, or my new home, were honeymoon-like in some ways. Not in the way of making love all hours of the day or in the way of being someplace exotic, but in the newness of the house and being with Liam in an environment that seemed to be jointly ours. Abraham kept to himself much of the time. I'd thought he'd be more present, but it was like he faded into the background when he wasn't needed.

As I rested on the sofa, Liam started the fireplace. It would be its first flame. It wasn't cool outside yet, but I wanted s'mores. No, I *needed* them… Thing 1 pushed under my ribs, while Thing 2 was lower and kicking outward, as if they both were pleading for me to feed them. My stomach couldn't rumble anymore—all my interior space was occupied, so hunger came to me without embarrassing gastric sounds.

Liam handed me a skewer with two marshmallows on its end.

"Graham crackers? Chocolate bars?"

"Give me a second." He went back to the kitchen and returned with an unwrapped Hershey's bar and four graham crackers on a plate, all lined up and awaiting their marshmallows.

"Perfection." I licked my lips and blew out the flaming top marshmallow. I topped my s'mores and covered the two sandwiches with a graham cracker.

We settled on the sofa together and watched the dancing flames as I filled my face with chocolaty gooeyness. Liam massaged my shoulders, his thumbs digging into the knots that grew under the strain of pregnancy. It couldn't get much better than this...

I ate every last crumb and was in the process of licking my fingers clean when the door rattled with a persistent knock. Liam looked at me with a furrowed brow. Abraham was in his room, and neither Shelby nor Danny would knock. They'd just let themselves inside. Liam was on his feet before I'd even considered standing up.

He looked through the glass before opening the door, but didn't look as if he knew the visitor. He shrugged in my direction before turning the knob. Then a familiar voice rang through the living room. *Mom*...

"Where's my daughter?"

I looked to the entry to see my mom coming toward me. She wheeled a bag behind her. Was that luggage? *Oh crap!* I hadn't seen her since Christmas, not that absence was a new thing for us. We were like oil and vinegar when we collided. I loved her because she hadn't done anything to make me feel otherwise, but liking her was another story. Her mothering skills were lax, especially after dad left us. I'd never blamed him, because it was like he disappeared into thin air. Now I understood better—he must have had to get away from her. I'd done the same in some ways by cutting her from my life. Holidays and birthdays were the only exceptions to our devoid relationship.

Mom's eyes locked on me as she drew near. Her weight shifted the sofa as she took Liam's spot. "When were you going to tell me that I was going to be a grandmother? After it's born, or maybe wait until it's off and grown?" She sniffled.

"It's not like that."

"Then what's it like, Elizabeth?"

"You know how we are…" I didn't want to say the obvious. Of course she knew how we were.

Mom shook her head and patted her bag. "Well, I'm here now. I guess that's all that matters."

I looked around for Liam, but he'd disappeared. "So you're staying? Here?"

"I've been through this before. You haven't. You'll want me around."

Not likely. I bit my tongue. I wouldn't say it… "Okay…" I rasped. What choice was there? Liam hadn't even stuck around to fight her off.

"Just how far along are you? Twelve months pregnant?"

I scowled. "I'm having twins."

Mom's eyes widened. "Good Lord! That explains your size at least."

I bit my tongue again, because there was no explaining the extra weight she carried.

Liam reappeared just in time to show Mom to our second guest room. Between her and Abraham, the house was filling up. Liam looked dangerous as he walked away with Mom, but she was bulletproof. It was him I worried about.

Chapter 7

Complications

Liam

With September came change. It wasn't all good. Hurricane Grace had landed, a.k.a Libby's mother. Grace said we would "need her help," but that was still yet to be proved. She wasn't like the mother I had known and learned by. No, she was like having an adult-sized child in the house, no help at all. She strained my every nerve to where her simple requests, like asking me to reach a dish on a high shelf, irritated me. It was apparent that Libby's looks must have come from her father's side of the family, thank God. Grace was plain and homely with straight, listless hair. Libby said her father had left them years ago, leaving Grace to be both mother and father. It seemed as if it was too much for one woman to do, at least for Grace.

"Liam!" Grace bellowed.

The twins' baby shower was today, which meant Grace was on a warpath. I'd cleaned and decorated and set out food, not wanting to see Libby climb a ladder or try to cook with the large baby bump she yielded, all while also accommodating Grace's demands.

"There you are. Where have you been hiding?" Grace laughed. "Could you break up the ice and put it in the ice bucket?"

It would still be an hour before guests arrived, and some ice would melt, but I did as she asked. "You better get yourself ready. You've only got an hour," I said in the hope that she would go somewhere else for a while.

Grace squinted at her thin brown leather wristwatch. "Oh, you're right." She shuffled out of the kitchen and toward the guest bathroom.

I went to check on Libby, who'd been resting most of the morning. The swelling in her ankles was worse than usual, and Abraham had ordered compression stockings, which had arrived the night before last, but Libby said her circulation was cut off when she wore them. I put them on her anyway.

"My calves looks like sausages in a casing!"

"Oh, stop it. You need to wear them, like it or not." Libby wasn't wrong, but there wasn't another option.

I pulled her up by her hands to sit on the edge of the bed.

"My head's spinning." She closed her eyes.

"Let it balance out." I held her shoulders so she wouldn't sway.

She rested her hands on my forearms. "I don't know how much longer I can be like this. I feel like my body is failing me." Her eyes were wet with tears. She joked about her growing body and its challenges, but this was the reality of it. *How much longer could she persist?*

"Shhh. I know it's a lot on you. At least we have Abraham on our side." We also had Grace, but…

She nodded, having heard my reassurances before. I tried, but I didn't know how her labor would work…it was terrifying.

She eased her way up and off of the mattress. I gripped her shoulders with more tension than necessary so she wouldn't fall.

"Ow!" Libby cried as she placed her hands under her belly. She breathed in and out like Abraham had taught her to do. "It's just round ligament pain." She massaged from under her belly and outward to her hip…the same hip she'd injured months back.

I walked with her to the bathroom and moved a chair in front of the vanity. Her breathing sounded too rapid, but it didn't stop her from doing her hair and makeup. I helped her into a capped sleeve dress that reached the floor. She still donned the compression stockings and would keep them on until bedtime.

"How do I look?" Libby smiled, but it looked pained.

"Beautiful." She was always beautiful. Her appearance had changed—her belly of course, her breasts were much larger, and she was swollen everywhere. She wore the sacrifices that she'd made for us. She suffered because of what I'd done. Because of me, her body was struggling to maintain both her pregnancy and her life, not to mention the pain she endured. With every passing day, it was getting harder to watch her put on a brave face.

The baby shower went better than I'd hoped. For fleeting moments, Libby forgot her pain. She laughed and opened scores of diapers and baby clothes in every shade of blue.

The idea to have the shower was all Grace's doing. I didn't know she had it in her, but she'd planned out every detail. The weird thing about Grace was that not everyone found her intolerable. In a social environment, she was almost as gracious as her name suggested. She had invited Shelby, Danny, Shelby's mother, Abraham, Libby's boss and coworkers, and a few of Libby's female relatives. In total, there were about fifteen people, and more than enough food. Grace couldn't be blamed for the food intolerances of some of the guests.

Danny carried in two matching hand-carved cribs one at a time. They were painted Kelly green and were the *pops* of color that Libby adored.

"Danny!" Libby stood to touch the cribs. "You've outdone yourself. How did you know I wanted green cribs?"

Danny nodded to Shelby. "Nothing gets past her. Shelby said this was what you wanted."

Libby hugged Danny. "Thank you. They're perfect!"

"I'll bring the dressers and changing table over tomorrow." Danny whispered to Libby but was still loud enough to hear. "I didn't want to steal the show." He winked and backed away to give the other guests an opportunity to see the cribs for themselves.

Once the guests left, I assisted Libby back to bed. I moved the cribs to the nursery, while Grace put the baby clothes in the closet.

Abraham began Libby's transfusion while she rested. I wished she'd have the same response to the blood that she'd initially had when she first began the transfusions. Now the added blood just made her cold. The buzz she used to get was also a thing of the past. I'd spoken to Abraham about upping the transfusions, but he thought it would do no good and would add too much volume and iron to her bloodstream. An added transfusion was still a possibility but would be postponed until its benefits outweighed its risks. The deficiency Libby suffered now wasn't a lack of nutrition but a lack of space left for the babies to grow.

The IV pump beeped once all of the blood had transfused. Abraham slipped into the bedroom and disconnected Libby, and then he slipped back out.

I helped Libby out of her dress and into a loose, silky peach-colored nightgown. Her dark nipples were visible through the thin material. I insisted that she cover up whenever Abraham came in, as I wanted to keep those images of her for myself. Her body was in full bloom. Her veins were prominent, and so was the permanent blush on her cheeks. She was ripe, but at the same time, a temptation that I couldn't have in any sense of the meaning.

"Help me up to the bathroom?" Her eyes were half-lidded as she kicked her legs to the side of the bed.

Libby massaged the sides of her belly before she stood. "My ribs hurt." I helped her to the edge of the bed, and as her legs dangled. Tears dripped from her eyes. "Ouch! It's really hurting!" Libby's voice was edged with panic that I hadn't heard before.

"Okay, I'll get Abraham."

"No, wait. I think it's all right." Libby eased off the bed into a standing position, and gushing water smacked onto the floor. "I think I've peed on myself." Her face flushed to a deep crimson.

Dripping down from her inner thighs was a stream of blood. The blood rushed down her leg and pooled in the floor. I didn't have time to explain, so I scooped her up and laid her back down on the bed. "Don't move!"

Abraham wasn't in his room, and so I ran outside screaming his name. The sun was still visible in the distance, though it was low to the horizon and about to set. He must have been to Danny's house, because I heard the rustle of underbrush, and then he emerged from the side yard. Abraham strode to my side, his expression wary.

"What is it?"

"Libby's bleeding." My throat constricted, and my voice cracked.

We both rushed back inside. Libby was crying and hyperventilating.

"Shhhh." I stroked her hair and whispered reassurances in her ear. *Not again. Please keep Libby alive.* I could not lose control. *Be strong...be strong...be strong...*

Modesty was pointless now. Libby was on the bed in her near transparent gown with her legs spread open. Blood saturated our quilt. *Just how much blood had she lost already?* Abraham examined her as he stood in the drying pool of blood on the floor. Abraham had brought over the ultrasound machine and was speaking to a colleague on his cell phone. I covered Libby's chest with an extra blanket, her teeth chattering, and her expression distant. Abraham gave Libby a sedative through the IV's hub.

The bleeding ebbed, and Libby's breathing regulated. Most of her respiratory problems stemmed from her panicked response, but I still felt dumbfounded as to what the real issue was. Abraham spoke excitedly on the phone. He seemed as scared as I was, but the ramifications would be different. He'd lose his confidence, whereas I'd lose everything.

***

Libby

Liam sat at the end of our bed, rubbing my feet. They ached all the time, even now that I was on bed rest. It was illogical. Abraham diagnosed the bleeding emergency as a marginal placenta previa. The diagnosis sounded terminal, but it happened because a part of the placenta covered the cervix. It could be dangerous, and I'd have to be cautious until the babies were far enough along to be delivered. Tomorrow I'd reach twenty-five weeks gestation and was now aiming for thirty-five weeks, when the babies should be developed enough for the cesarean. Intimacy between Liam and me was nonexistent. He took care of me, but it lacked something vital, though the urge to be bitten returned. I tried to blow it off, but that same urge sat in my every thought like a coiled snake.

Liam's need for blood doubled since I was on bed rest. He seemed to think that he needed to be by my side every waking moment, which only made him yearn for blood more. He didn't think that I'd picked up on his trembling fingers or frequent escapes to feed, but I wasn't blind. I hadn't told him about my sick obsession returning either. He was thirsty, and I wanted to be tasted... It was a dangerous combination. Liam excused himself from the room. In his place came my mom, as if I needed a sitter.

"How are you feeling today, baby?" Mom said as she plopped on the bed beside me.

My body moved with the wake of her less-than-graceful landing. "Fine." I tried to interject as much cheer as I could, but my voice fell flat.

"Well, you're filling out nicely anyways." Mom patted my enlarged belly.

"Thanks..." My body resembled a gigantic turtle that was shell bound. I thought about it enough without needing any reminders.

"You know what I mean." She looked me over again. "Just wait for the stretched-out skin and hemorrhoids," Mom said without missing a beat.

Besides, I already had skin that couldn't give much more before it stretched thin enough to resemble an x-ray fish.

"Holy hell, Mom. Why would you say that?" This is why we didn't get along. She was always quick to find negative things to focus on. As it stood, I could come up with enough negativity on my own.

"Well, I made out just fine when I had you. I'm sure you'll do just as well."

It wasn't that I didn't love my mom. I did, but following in her footsteps wasn't what I wanted. She always complained. Her arthritis was severe, but who wanted to hear about her aches and pains all the time?

"Are you sure that it's safe for Abraham and his team to perform a cesarean here?" Mom whispered. This wasn't her first attempt at bashing the plan, but she didn't know the whole story. I couldn't go to a normal hospital and get the care that I'd receive here. The human world wouldn't know what they were dealing with. Surgery scared me no matter where it took place.

"Perfectly safe. I'll also be less likely to contract an infection here. You know how germy hospitals are." I forced a smile and tried to look confident.

Mom patted my hand. "Okay then…" She sounded unconvinced.

When lunchtime rolled around, Mom left to the kitchen to fix us something to eat. When she returned, it was evident she wouldn't be happy until I ate my weight in fried food. Liam usually prepared my meals, but since I was under my mom's charge, I'd eat to satisfy her. I managed to consume three chicken wings, French fries, and baked beans topped with bacon. My stomach was bloated, and heartburn surged. At last Abraham came in, and my mom scooted out of his way.

"I'll be in the kitchen cleaning up if you need me." Mom left and shut the door behind her. Maybe she'd never open it again. I wouldn't be that lucky.

"You look green," Abraham said as a greeting.

"Is it that obvious?" My stomach knotted.

"I don't think that your mom is the best person to feed you." Abraham grinned. His cheeks reddened to match his dark-red hair.

"I think that she was trying to kill me." Abraham gave me a dose of Mylanta, which seemed to ease the bloating as it coated my stomach.

Abraham's face grew more serious. "How are you holding up, Libby?"

I considered what he was asking, and tears formed in my eyes. I hadn't intended on crying, but pregnancy hormones turned my conviction to mush. "I'm scared."

Abraham sat down beside me on the bed and put his arms around me. He was more than a doctor. He was my friend.

"It's tricky, no doubt, but there will be plenty of support staff during your delivery."

"I know…" Knowing didn't make it any easier. *This could kill me.* The door cracked opened.

Liam stood in the doorway. "Was I interrupting something?"

Abraham's arms dropped away, which only made our embrace look guilty despite its innocence.

"If you'll excuse me." Abraham left without another word.

Liam sat on the edge of our bed. "I think Abraham has feelings for you." His voice was gruff.

"You know that he's a friend. Don't be jealous." How could he be jealous? As if I would ever want anyone else.

"I don't like how he looks at you. Maybe it's irrational, but if he wasn't your doctor…" Liam looked away.

"He looks at me like I'm going to die." I wasn't naive enough to believe anything else.

"You're not going to die."

"Said the immortal." I scowled and met his eyes.

"You say that like it's a blessing. You know it's not."

"Right now it looks like salvation to me." Would he even change me? It couldn't happen until after the babies were delivered. I would need a plan, but there were only two people I could ask to change me, and I didn't know if Liam was even up for that task. As much as I loved him, sacrificed for him, why didn't he love me enough to change me?

Liam kissed my forehead. "I don't want you to give up. Seeing you like this kills me, you know, and when you talk like that... Damn it, Libby. What am I supposed to say?"

"You know what I want."

"You still have time. Don't give up on your options yet. It's not like you have no other choice." Liam held me tight, as if I'd slip through his hands.

"I'm betting that I don't have as much time as you think." I paused. "If I were dying, would you change me?"

Liam took a deep breath. "Without a second thought."

"That's what I'm betting on..." Either way, it would happen, even if he didn't know it yet.

***

Libby

Still bedridden at thirty-two weeks pregnant. Almost every spot on my back aches. Bed rest is painful. At this point I should be tough and calloused, but that had yet to happen. Most of my days and nights had been spent cat napping. Pregnancy and stagnation seemed to work around the clock to exhaust me.

Cold touches my skin, hot breath feathers my face, and moans escape from Liam as he pulls off my clothes. I turn my neck, tempting him. He takes the bait. My skin is pierced, and pleasure incites, at last. I groan his name as I hold him to me. He won't deny me now…

"Libby, Libby."

I gasped as I was shook awake. "Are you okay? You were making strange noises." Abraham is shirtless and is only wearing sleep pants. His abdominal muscles ripple in perfection.

"What?" I turn to look for Liam, but his side of the bed is empty. "I was just dreaming."

"Okay then. I'll be back in a while."

"What time is it?" My eyes were still sleep blind.

"Just past sunrise. Six ten."

Liam would already be up to feed. "Sorry to worry you."

"It's my job." Abraham winked and left.

There was a tattoo on his back. Who knew? It was centered between his shoulder blades and showed a totem pole of sorts, but it was of animal heads. It was sexy on him, so unexpected.

Liam joined me seconds later. He sniffed the air as if he was trying to pin down a scent.

"What was Abraham doing in here half-naked?"

Was he serious? "He heard me dreaming, and thought something was wrong."

"He shouldn't walk around like that," he mumbled.

"I was dreaming of you."

"What was it about?" His expression eased.

"Sexual gratification. That's what I was dreaming about."

"My only need is that you and the boys are safe. The rest can wait."

"You don't think that's on my mind every second of the day? Not a minute goes by that I'm not aware of the danger. Not a single minute…"

Liam's large hand caressed my bulging belly. "You three are my world. If one of you is lost, I'll be lost too." His words were sweet, but I craved action.

Once the sun was up a little higher in the sky, Liam left to go over some business with Danny. Abraham came in to do his morning assessments.

"Sorry about earlier." He was dressed now in jeans and a polo. He looked nice, but it did no justice for the body that was underneath of his loose polo.

"There's nothing to be sorry for." I pulled my shirt up, anticipating his next move.

He measured my growth and palpated for the lie of the babies before listening to them with a Doppler. The thudding of twin A's heart filled the room, as did twin B's when the Doppler was set over his heart. "They're doing remarkably well. Good job."

I'd need names soon. Twin A and B lacked something. "Thanks." Should I ask him now? If not now, then when? Sweat pricked on my forehead. I had to have a backup plan. But would he do it? "Listen. Abraham, I have a favor to ask you."

His expression looked wry as he met my gaze. Did he know what I was going to ask? "Okay?"

"After the babies are delivered, I want to be changed…" My voice was almost inaudible.

"And…"

"I think Liam will do it, but if he doesn't, would you think about doing it for me?"

"Libby…" His voice was kind. "I couldn't imagine going behind Liam's back. Don't you know how hurt he'd be or what he'd think? My God, he'd want vengeance."

Tears fell on my cheeks. "So that's a no then?" I held back breathless sobs. *Please leave…*

Instead he pulled a chair close to the bedside. "Give him time to come around to the idea. If all else fails, then I'll consider it. But I wouldn't do it unless Liam was already aware. I couldn't do that to him."

The scuffle of mom's slippers made me stiffen. I dried my face and tried to look like I hadn't been crying. The door opened inward without a knock.

"How's she today, Doc?" Mom asked. Her hair was in curlers, and she wore a modest blouse, capris, and freakin' support hose that didn't look much different than the ones I had on.

"She's doing well, aren't you, Libby?" Abraham was back to his professional persona, all traces of our affinity gone.

"When I carried Libby, I had to get a lot of blood transfusions too. Do you think it's genetic?"

Why am I just hearing about this now?

"You did?" Abraham's interest seemed heightened.

"I lived in Stockton then. Maybe it was the county doctor treatment of the time?" Mom sat down on the side of the bed and grunted when she plopped by my side.

Abraham rubbed his chin. "Perhaps… Were you told why you were given transfusions? It's not a standard method of treatment, not even back then."

Mom stared across the room and tapped her finger on her knee. "Well, no, but I was so sick starting off. My husband called in the doctor, and after that I was fine. The transfusions perked me up and made pregnancy as comfortable as it could be for the time. My morning sickness had been so bad that I thought I'd die."

"Maybe it's genetics, like you said." Abraham checked my IV tubing one more time. "I'll be on the deck if you need me, Libby. I have a few calls I need to make."

What did it mean? After all this time, Mom couldn't have even once mentioned the odd transfusions she'd received?

"My knee is killing me, Lib. I pray that you don't get as bad off as I am. It's terrible to get old."

***

Liam

Thoughts, worries, anticipation, hysteria, fear, dread… *What did it all mean? Was I losing my mind?* Stupid, that was what it was. Abraham was harmless. Instead of chastising him, I should be praising him. He was the only thread that linked Libby to life. I'd cast her to brimstone by fulfilling my stupid whims, or was it lust? I couldn't think, or even give Libby what she needed—affection. I cared for her, but not in the way she required. Libby wasn't like any other women. She was one of a kind, and I was going to lose her if I didn't wake up.

The forest was calm, but a devious wind pushed itself through the trees. I'd attacked a squirrel, of all things. It was akin to eating one grape, a pointless act. After weaving through the trees over an hour, I knelt by Ciara's Celtic cross headstone. The memorial was one thing I'd done right. She would've approved. I brushed away leaf remnants from the top of the Bianco marble. The stone was smooth and cold as death. What remained of Ciara under earth and stone? Other than this marker, it was as if nothing of her endured, which was the way it should be. I hadn't meant to force this life on her, but what did I know at the time? Nothing, that was what. Sometimes I'd come here to talk to Ciara as if she were still alive. She was my voice of reason, if not my reason for living. I'd taken her for granted and worked her like an employee. Our shared mission had been survival. It was gritty, hard, and dirty, but she didn't shy away from our lot, even if it was her downfall. Would I have survived this long without her? I couldn't guess. I liked the challenge being a vampire posed, but would that have been enough? Now Libby talked as if this was what she wanted too. She was my treasure, but did I want to be around indefinitely? *Lord...*

"What do I do? Just tell me. Please!" My fingers trembled, and my voice shook. Nothing happened at first, but then my stomach clenched. Unnatural queasiness gripped me, and my eyes teared. "What?" Perched on top of the cross was a cloudy likeness of Ciara. Vitality shown in her eyes, and gone was the harsh set of her mouth. She wore a pale frock that hugged her dainty curves. "Ciara?" I mouthed. My sanity was further gone than I'd thought.

"It's fine, Liam. I'm well." Ciara's words were as clear as if she were still living.

"What are you doing here?" I stood to meet her, delusion or not.

"I had to let you know that I'm all right. You need to let me go completely. It's your only hope."

I reached to touch her skin, but my fingers passed through her. The air around her was chilly and cooler than the surrounding forest. "Forgive me, but I've already let you go."

"I don't mean of my physical body. I mean of the blame that you put on yourself. It weighs you down. Surely you see it does?"

Her hair flowed over her shoulders and halfway down her back in pecan-brown ripples. She was more beautiful now than she'd ever been.

"Don't you see, Ciara? You suffered because of me. You had to live this curse because of me."

"Do I look cursed now?"

She didn't. She was perfection. "I loved you, Ciara."

"You loved me the only way you knew how. It wasn't enough, but that wasn't your fault. You couldn't have saved me no matter what you did. I didn't want saving. I wanted salvation…"

"You have it now, don't you?" I wiped tears from my eyes. Maybe I couldn't have saved her, but I'd needed to try.

"You can see that I do. I'm where I've always wanted to be and doing what I was always supposed I'd do. We were great together as…friends. I'm sorry if my words hurt you. I never wanted to hurt you, Liam. I loved you the best I could have at the time."

The wind rushed through my hair, but Ciara's remained in place.

"What do I do then?"

"You do what's required. I think you know what the answer is already."

"I don't want to hurt Libby like I did you. What we had was ruined in that one act."

"You're wrong. My life was prolonged but not ruined. Libby isn't like me, but I'm sure you know that. You and I weren't on the same track. We tried to force it, but it was doomed from the start. I should have told you going in where my loyalties were. Maybe we wouldn't have wed? I don't know. There isn't a right path. Any path you land on is the right path, and it eventually leads you to where you were supposed to be all along. I can't tell you why we were put together for so long, but I do know this—I've ended up right where I was supposed to be. Timing seems to be irrelevant."

"Libby wants me to change her. I don't think she realizes what she's asking."

"I can't tell you what to do. There are no hard and steady rules to follow."

"I don't know what to do…" Talking with Ciara was always easy. That could've been why we got on like we did for so long.

"All I can say is to love her. In the end, it's all that matters." The lines and planes of Ciara's form weakened as she diffused in front of my eyes. I reached out again to touch her, but all that remained was a swirl of mist that went into nothingness.

I sat back down by the grave. Was any of that real, or was it all imagined? After a time, I brushed off my pants and walked back home. It didn't matter if I had dreamt it all, because the guilt that had gripped me since Ciara's death had eased. That had to mean something…

Chapter 8

Medical Mayhem

Libby

Thirty-four weeks down, thank God and praise the Lord… The end was edging closer every day. Shelby perched on the end of my bed with a bottle of Essie nail polish that was called Fishnet Stockings. This was the closest I'd been to wearing anything sexy in months. The deep-crimson polish made my toes sparkle and look less like boiled hotdogs.

"Are your reservations confirmed for Fiji yet? I wish I could go somewhere exotic too…" On December 11, she'd be a Mrs. and would jet off to a private island in Fiji. She'd moved the wedding to before Christmas because it conflicted with the honeymoon suite's availability. Meanwhile, I'd be tending to my babies. My plans weren't bad, but they sounded rather mundane.

"Yes! First class all the way!" Shelby squealed. She capped the polish and sprayed a fast-drying solution, which smelled like coconut, over my toes.

This was as happy as I'd ever seen her. "You'll be gone for how long?"

"Two weeks. The hut is over the water. I meant to bring over the brochure. You'd die."

"Maybe you could bring it to me later. I'm so sick of TV reruns. I need something new to look at."

"Aren't you meeting with the labor-and-delivery team today? Where are they going to stay?"

"They'll be here anytime. I think Abraham said they'd come in travel trailers. They take their homes with them state to state."

"Well, I guess I'll see them coming, or hear them."

"True story."

Shelby tidied my room and dry dusted the floors throughout the house. I couldn't tell how dusty the house had gotten, since I lived in bed. My mom did the laundry and ran the dishwasher, but nothing in depth.

Toward the late afternoon, a cacophony of motors and vehicle sounds roared. Through the window were five travel trailers lining up in a makeshift travel semicircle. It looked like a band of gypsies had descended.

"They're coming." Liam sat by my side and pulled me closer. Was he nervous too? This was almost as stressful on him as on me. A new horde of people scrambling around would only add to the havoc.

He nuzzled my ear and whispered, "I love you." He'd finally come around. I wasn't his patient, or even worse, his victim. I was his equal, though I still couldn't tell what that meant.

The bedroom door was half-open, and strange footsteps echoed throughout the living room. A knock on the door made me jump. Liam held me tighter. Abraham peered inside the bedroom, and Liam nodded.

"Libby, Liam, I'd like for you to meet the concierge team. They'll be around until after delivery." Abraham led the group into our bedroom. They faced us, and it was easy to tell the pediatricians and their nurses from the rest of the group—they were the only humans. The glossy-haired, blemish-free group could've been models, whereas the humans, not so much.

"Thank you all for coming." Liam looked in the direction of each and every new face.

"The anesthesiologist is still en route but will be here by the evening." Abraham gestured to a tall man and woman, both donned in lab coats and expensive-looking shoes. "This is Frank and Ida Morton. Frank is a surgeon and general practitioner, and his wife, Ida, has a doctorate in nursing." Abraham then motioned toward two lanky men with salt-and-pepper hair. "This is Jim, a respiratory therapist, as is his brother, Henry." The shorter man named Henry elbowed Jim in the ribs. Henry was attractive but looked more normal than the rest of the vampires. "And on this other end is the pediatrics team. Dr. Louis Stein, Dr. Amy Potter, nurse Lynne Brown, and last but not least, nurse Valerie Ayers."

"It's so nice to meet you all." Is this how it felt to be abducted by aliens? They all gave me curious glances and would get a shot at poking and prodding me. This was going to be great…

My mom's slippers shuffled past the door. I wouldn't come in either if I were her.

Abraham spoke to the group. "I've worked with most of this team before. If anything is needed, please come and find me. My room is upstairs to the left." Abraham turned to me. "Maybe you wouldn't mind if Dr. Morton examines you later?"

My pulse quickened. This wasn't how I liked meeting new people. "Of course."

"Just as a reminder. The cesarean is tentatively planned for Sunday. Libby will be thirty-five weeks on the nose and will receive additional transfusions up until delivery, along with IV fluids."

Liam remained by my side for Dr. Morton's exam. Dr. Morton wore such a serious expression that goose bumps dotted my arms and legs. Abraham was here too, but the vibe of the room was more intense than it'd ever been.

"Breathe," Liam whispered.

Dr. Morton glided the ultrasound wand over my slick belly. He jotted notes and said very little. Abraham dried my belly with a towel. Maybe Dr. Morton was used to having an assistant?

"The boys look fine. I'm estimating that they will each weigh at least five pounds at birth."

"Thank you, Doctor," I said.

The doctors left our bedroom, shutting the door behind them. There'd be no privacy until these babies were out. Liam tickled along my belly and kissed me behind my ear. Sex was out of the question, but my body didn't know that. I wanted him so much that I cramped.

"You're killing me, you know."

"I'm sorry. You're just too tempting."

I'd made it this far along, and he'd been the strong one. *What gives?*

"One bite. That's all. Don't ask me again." His voice was low and husky. His hazel eyes flickered like a candle's flame.

"I won't." If I said too much, he'd change his mind. The assault of his mouth was slow and deliberate. He kissed me like he'd been denied my touch. He nibbled my ear, and his cool lips trailed down my neck. The puncture was quick and painless. He held me in place, and I lost my cool and moaned. Thank God the door was shut. Tension that had snaked itself in my body dropped away. All complaints and discomforts gone... Like a jolt of electricity or a lightbulb suddenly turning on, I remembered the first bite, my eclipsed memory now restored.

***

The second blood transfusion of the day coursed into my arm. It was still hidden with a paper bag over the actual bag of blood and shielded with colored tubing. Feeding on blood had to be different than having it pumped like gasoline into a car. I pushed aside my dinner tray, having eaten over half of what was piled on it to begin with. The vegetable beef soup and buttered French bread was good, but I could only fit so much in my stomach at a time. The day seemed to drag on forever with the arrival of the concierge team. Abraham said he'd bring by the anesthesiologist if he wasn't too late arriving.

Liam had slipped out. There were too many people around for him. He needed a breather.

Just after nine, someone knocked on my door.

"Come in."

Abraham walked in with another man. The other man was tall, well built, and he looked to be in his midthirties, with blond hair, and eyes the same blue as mine. My breath caught. *Could it be?* Was I hallucinating? This shouldn't be possible.

"Libby, this is the anesthesiologist, Dr. Kent Anderson."

I stared at Kent Anderson… He stared back, his expression horrified. He wasn't a day over thirty-five and looked better than he had the last time I'd seen him. This was where I got my looks from. He was why I had such a hard time in relationships, and he was why I was raised by a single mom. Abraham looked back and forth between us, confusion marring his perfect face.

"Dad." There was no mistaking him, and not a doubt in my mind of his identity.

"Come again?" Abraham's cheeks were blotchy. He had to see the resemblance.

"Can I speak with Libby alone?" Kent addressed Abraham, but his gaze remained on me.

"Is that okay, Libby?" Abraham seemed hesitant.

"Yes, thank you, Abraham." My voice was quiet, like a child's. Maybe that was the only voice Kent would've remembered. Abraham left, shutting the door behind him. Kent stood at the end of my bed, unmoving. It'd been too long since he left. What was there even to say?

"I didn't know you were the patient. I should've checked your chart, but I thought if I kept my head down, no one would notice me here."

"Would you have come if you knew?" Maybe he didn't want to see me, as if my childhood had been too much to bear?

"Yes, but with more discretion."

I took a deep breath. This wasn't how I'd imagined seeing my dad again. I thought that he'd come back to me someday, but not as an obligation. I was a patient, a requirement of his job.

"Was there ever a plan to see me again?"

"I didn't think it would be in your best interest when you were a child." His eyes looked pleading, but his tone was numb.

"You thought that I'd be better off raised by a single mother? She didn't have anything, or time to spend with me. You didn't even send her money to help raise me. Why, Dad…why?"

"You know why I couldn't keep in touch. Grace…your mother never knew about me or what I was."

"You married her."

"I fooled myself into thinking that she didn't have to know, but I was wrong. She was suspicious, and it was easier for me to disappear than to explain myself. I'm sorry. Grace had you to keep from being lonely. I would've just been a complication for you both. I have to believe that." Tears edged his eyes, but they didn't fall. "I wish I would've chosen differently now."

"Just so you know, my childhood wasn't easy. We didn't have much, and you know how Mom is…"

"It's too late for me to have done anything differently. I've been on my own since I left, if that's any consolation."

"Mom's here, you know."

His face blanched.

"She can't know I'm here. Does she know about your husband?"

"Liam and I aren't married yet, and no, she doesn't know."

"You can't tell her. It'd destroy her, and I've already done enough as far as she's concerned."

"I won't tell her. What good would it do anyway? It's bad enough that I know what you are, and you didn't love her enough to change her yourself."

"It wasn't that I didn't love her. She wouldn't have understood. Very few people can wrap their brains around it. It's illogical at best."

"What about me then? I know what you are…"

He eased a little and sat down in the chair near the bed. "You have my DNA. There was no way you wouldn't have come around eventually." He rubbed his chin. "I wanted to come back for you, but knew that you'd be better off with your mom. I was right. Look at you now."

"Damn it, Dad…" I sniffled back tears that blurred my vision and made my nose run. "What do we do now?" Mom had to be in the dark, yet Abraham already knew.

"I can dodge your mom as long as my identity is under wraps." He offered his hand for me to hold, and I grabbed it. The last time I'd held his hand, I was a little girl. I still needed him.

"We'll keep things quiet. It's the only way." He squeezed my hand. His hand was large and reassuring, like a dad's hand should be.

"I really am sorry for not being around. I've lived like a nomad. It's been for the best." He paused. "Someday I'll make it up to you. I don't know how, but I will."

I nodded. If I spoke now, my walls would crumble. There'd be no way for him to overlook that. He stood and kissed my forehead before he left.

I'd always thought he'd ran off with another woman. I'd imagined that he had another family too…

***

Liam

Libby's jaw was slack with earned slumber. Delivery was only days away, but until then she'd need as much rest as could be granted. I showered and slipped into bed by her side.

Early-morning rustling from the kitchen woke me. It didn't take much to wake me, but Libby's eyes were already open in our semidark bedroom.

"What time is it?" she asked in a hoarse tone.

I glanced at the clock that rested on my bedside table. "Just after seven. Are you hungry?"

She nodded. I kissed her forehead, knowing that she'd refuse a mouth kiss before she'd brushed her teeth. I brought over the wheeled table that held her makeup and toiletries and went into the kitchen. It took her a while to focus in the mornings, not that she was ever a morning person to begin with.

Abraham sat at the kitchen table reading the *Daily Times* newspaper. At least he remembered to put on a shirt this morning. The coffeemaker was steaming with fresh brew. The scent of it stimulated my senses, but the taste of coffee wasn't what I savored. He looked up from the opened newspaper. "How's Libby holding up?"

"Fine, but tired."

"I meant from last night."

His expression was serious. Just what had happened last night?

"You'll have to elaborate."

"Oh. Perhaps I shouldn't have said anything. I'm sorry." Abraham folded his newspaper and set it on the table.

"What happened?"

Abraham stood as if about to make his escape, but he wouldn't leave without spilling whatever the secret was.

"It's probably best if you hear it from Libby. It concerns her, after all."

"Just tell me."

Abraham cleared his throat and looked side to side. "Her father is here," he whispered.

"What do you mean, he's here?" He was an absent father at best. Why would he return?

"He's the anesthesiologist. Dr. Anderson didn't know that Libby was the patient."

"Who else knows?" If Grace found out, it'd be chaos. "Wait a minute. Is he like us?"

Abraham nodded. I pushed my fingers back in my hair and paced around the kitchen. *Great...*

"If you'll excuse me." Abraham turned for the stairs, but I grabbed his arm before he was out of my reach.

"We'll have to keep this quiet. You know, Grace."

"Of course."

Libby hadn't said a thing, but she'd been half-asleep when I'd left her. I cooked a quick spinach omelet and put it on a tray, along with a glass of cranberry juice. I held in the secret as Libby ate. She finished most of the meal and pushed away the rest.

"Liam…"

I took her hand.

"Abraham already told me."

A stray tear fell onto her cheek. "He left because he didn't want to explain himself to my mom."

Would I have taken the same path if I didn't have Danny and Shelby around? No… "It's not easy sharing the truth. Especially when you know how ridiculous it sounds." I didn't want to give excuses for him, but the reality of it rang true.

"I know, but it would've been nice to have a father around." She rested her head against my shoulder.

At least I'd be around for our boys.

"How is it between you and your dad now?"

"It still hurts. The fact that he moved on without us isn't easy to get past, but…he's still my dad." Libby wiped her eyes. "Mom can't know. It'd wreck her, but I want him around."

She was a daddy's girl who'd been without a dad for too long. "Okay, we'll keep it quiet."

During the late afternoon, a surgical bed, two incubators, various monitors, and other surgical instruments arrived. The pediatric nurses laid a thick plastic matting on the living room floor after the sofa and chairs were moved to the loft. The room smelled of bleach and plastic. Abraham directed Danny and me to move the equipment and bed in place. The nurses calibrated the equipment to assure that all were functional. A backup generator was connected to the medical equipment. Nothing could be left to chance or malfunction.

I finally had the chance to knock on the door of the Coachmen Mirada. The exterior of the RV was a glossy swirl design of tan, brown, and black. A blond-haired man opened the door. His hair was darker than Libby's chemically lightened locks, but his nose and chin were so much like his daughter's.

"Dr. Anderson?" My voice was acidic, but I'd come for Libby's sake. Her father's intentions were yet to be determined.

He reached out to shake my hand and gestured for me to come inside. I stepped into the RV. The living area was more spacious than I'd thought possible, and the leather sofa and dining built-ins were top quality.

"Have a seat."

We faced each other from opposite ends of the sofa.

"I'm Liam." My palms began to sweat as I realized that I was actually with Libby's father and that he was just as durable as I was. He'd never grow old and die.

"You can call me Kent." He reclined back onto the sofa in a more comfortable-looking position. "I assume that you know who I am?"

"Libby's father." He dressed like me and was surrounded by a modest yet nice house.

"I don't want my ex-wife, Grace, finding me. She wouldn't understand."

"Yes, a low profile is in your best interest." My courage grew. He wasn't a threat, but more of an unplanned obstacle. "What happens after the babies are born? Will you disappear again?"

"I haven't thought that far ahead. I'd like to keep in touch with Libby, but I'll leave that decision for her to make."

I nodded. "Will she be able to contact you?"

His eyes softened and looked genuine, as Libby looked when she wore that same expression. "I'd like that, but I don't want to force myself in her life after all that I've missed."

Maybe he wasn't the bad guy after all. "How old are you, Kent?"

"I was changed just before my thirty-seventh birthday, but chronologically, I'm in my eighties." He rolled his eyes, a classic Libby move. "I was swept up in the early hippie movement. One night everything changed, including what I was. I was always mild natured, but one night of abandon helped me to grow up. I didn't know what happened at first, but then was sent to my sire. His name was Teddy. He gave me direction and helped me to adapt. I finished medical school, opting for anesthesiology as my main focus. I worked as a hospital administrator when I was married to Grace. The hours were more stable, and I was home on the weekends. After I left, the schedule didn't matter anymore."

I didn't want to admit it, but I struggled with a life that Kent had already faced. It seemed as if he failed the most vital part, but still, he was a vampire that had fathered a child. "Any words of wisdom?"

"Don't mess it up like I did. If you can do that, everything else will work out."

Now, how not to mess things up?

***

Libby

One day left… I could get out of bed and get the baby things together, but I'd been warned not to move, not when I'd made it this far. Instead, Shelby readied the cribs by putting navy-and-white striped sheets on the mattresses, stocked the diaper holder, and made it so that everything I'd need would be close by. The boys would stay in our bedroom until I could walk around like a normal human being. How long would that be with abdominal surgery? Maybe the change to vampire would help me heal faster? I wouldn't broach the subject of my change until the babies were both out and well.

"How's this?" Shelby had the cribs side by side with the changing table in the middle.

"Perfect." I held my side and grimaced. "Braxton Hicks…" The contractions had intensified over the past two days, but labor hadn't started. I took a deep breath as the pain lessened.

Shelby picked up two puffy blue winter bunny suits. "These are from Mom."

"Could you write those in the baby books? I'll want to send her a thank-you card."

"You don't have to do that." Shelby flipped open the baby books.

"I've got to keep up with this stuff. Your mom is old school. She'll be offended if she's not properly thanked."

"Have it your way," Shelby muttered. Etiquette wasn't her thing, but it was the one thing I excelled at. Shelby's mom was more of a mother than Grace had been. Janice was warm and caring, the kind of mother I wanted to be.

"I saw baby tuxedos online. Would you let the boys wear them to my wedding?"

"Of course I would."

"Good, because they're already ordered."

Had I rubbed off on her that much?

Kent came in the house to check his equipment and had poked his head around the door. He wore a face mask with the excuse of being as germ-free as possible, but it was really his disguise. Mom shuffled by the living room while he was at his equipment, and she didn't look up even once. I hadn't told Shelby about Kent. She wouldn't have remembered him, since he'd left when I was young, and there was no pressing reason to tell her either. The less people in on the secret, the easier it was to lie about who he was.

With all preparations made for the delivery, I had my last meal just after six. I'd want an empty stomach for tomorrow. Anxiety slowed my appetite. There was little doubting that my stomach would be empty enough for surgery.

"Come on, baby." Liam helped me to the already filled bathtub. I was on bed rest but could walk to the bathroom.

"I'm not ready for this." I dropped my robe and held Liam's hand as I stepped into the tub. It was warm and smelled like lavender.

"You're not ready for the bath or the babies?"

I rolled my eyes in his direction, which he didn't see. "The delivery. The more I think about it, the more barbaric it seems."

Liam soaked the washcloth and wiped my face. "Do you think Abraham, or any of the doctors, are going to intentionally harm you? Do you think your dad would allow it?"

"No, but you have to admit the logistics are terrifying."

"It's the safest way for you to deliver. I know that you're scared, but it's your best bet."

"You're going to be there, aren't you?" Or would my blood be too much for him?

"I'll hold your hand the entire time." He washed my body, and I dipped my head back to wet my hair. My mom would sit it out. Liam was the only one who could calm me. I'd need him there. Thank God he would be by my side. He helped me to rinse the shampoo out of my hair, and he pulled me up from the water by my hands. I was slick as a seal and distorted by a twin pregnancy, but there was still longing in his eyes for me.

"Ouch!" I supported my side as Braxton Hicks contractions spasmed and knotted. Liam scooped me into his arms and took my saturated body to the bed, where he patted me off with a dry towel.

"Your suffering will soon be over." I let him comb out my knotty hair, help me into my gown, and wrap me in the bed. I trusted him with my life— surrender was now.

Chapter 9

Tidal Wave

Liam

At five in the morning, the surgical team scurried around the house like rodents. I'd hoped that Libby could sleep, but that was futile. Grace had voiced her concerns and had already been awake, annoying the surgical team. She was scared that things would go south, and then what? That was my first concern, but if there was danger, Libby would be safer here than in the best human hospital available. This wasn't a run-of-the-mill labor-and-delivery unit, and every contingency had been planned.

Libby refused to look like a patient, and she had styled her hair and was still in the process of applying makeup as I paced around our bedroom looking for things to do to keep my hands busy. I tidied the room as Libby finished her makeup. Normally I'd work, but my concentration was gone. I'd lose money and maybe even clients if I worked under this pressure.

"Is the camera charged?" Libby asked with wide eyes as she drew on eyeliner.

"Yes, it's all ready to go."

The door shoved open. Grace, not fully dressed yet, carried a small box in her hand. She sat by Libby. "I want you to wear this." Grace opened the box and removed the necklace that rested inside. "I wore this when you were born. It was from your father. It's for good luck." Libby moved her hair aside as Grace fastened the clasp.

"Thanks, Mom." Libby's eyes were teary. Grace sniffled and hugged her daughter.

"You're welcome." Grace stood to leave. "I'll see you and the boys soon." Grace weaved through the surgical area and headed back to her room. Once dressed, she'd go over to Danny's house.

I grabbed the camera and snapped a candid of Libby. We'd forget this once the boys were here.

"Hey!" Libby's eyes were red rimmed.

"You're beautiful—don't worry."

Abraham knocked and entered our room. "We're ready for you."

I helped Libby to the bathroom and heard Danny in the living room. He'd been charged with driving Grace to his house. It was a short walk, but Grace's knees weren't up for it. She'd be his responsibility for the day.

Once Libby was ready, I walked by her side to the living room. Nothing about this room looked the same. It had been transformed from our home to a new-age hospital suite. Blinding fluorescent lighting surrounded the bed and equipment. Nothing escaped their illumination. The pediatricians and their nurses were on the other side by the incubators. The respiratory therapist team was near the pediatric area and were ready with suction machines and oxygen.

The Mortons' were by the surgical bed, along with Kent. Everyone was covered in surgical clothes from head to toe.

I helped Libby to the side of the bed. Mrs. Morton placed fetal monitors on Libby's belly. Her blood pressure was checked, and Kent opted to give Libby a spinal anesthetic.

"Will it hurt?" Libby whispered to her dad.

"Not bad, and even then, you'll only feel a pinch."

I supported Libby as Kent prepped her back and administered the needle into her spine. Hushed cries filled my ears.

"Shhhh… The worst is almost over." I hoped. I held her in place minutes more until her balance became unsteady. Mrs. Morton directed me on how to position Libby. An oxygen nasal cannula was put in Libby's nose.

Mrs. Morton took Libby's wrist and strapped it down to the wing of the bed. She did the same on the other side. I watched in horror, not understanding the protocol.

"I don't like this." Libby was breathing too fast. She pulled on the restraints. I unfastened them. After Sam's attack, restraints were out of the question for Libby.

Mr. Morton scowled at me. "I've got her." I sat by Libby's head and was able to loop my arms under hers. She'd be fine.

Abraham blocked our view with a drape that extended upward from Libby's rib cage.

Mrs. Morton prepped Libby's belly. I looked over the drape to see Dr. Morton with his scalpel in hand. I sat all the way back down and tried not to breathe. Her blood would be in the air soon enough.

"Can you feel anything, Libby?" Dr. Morton said through his mask.

Libby's face looked panicked but not pained. "No. I don't think so."

Over the drape, Dr. Morton peered down. "You'll feel pressure when the babies are extracted, but there shouldn't be pain."

Libby nodded.

"Okay, Libby. We're beginning," Abraham said from where he stood just opposite of Dr. Morton.

I hugged Libby tighter. "I love you. You're doing great."

Libby's eyes were closed so tightly that the skin around her eyes was blanched. I caressed the side of her cheek. "Don't forget to breathe."

Kent bent down by Libby's other side. "Okay, Libby. In and out. Now isn't the time to hold your breath. Your babies will still need oxygen."

Libby kept her eyes closed, but she breathed. Her body moved as the first baby was freed. It squeaked out muffled reassuring cries.

"It's a boy!" Abraham held the baby over the drape so that we could see him. Libby opened her eyes.

A loud cry bellowed after Jim, the lankier respiratory therapist, suctioned the baby's airway. My son didn't cease crying as one nurse toweled him dry while the other assessed his condition.

"His Apgar is a nine at one minute," said the older-looking nurse loud enough for the entire pediatric team to hear.

Dr. Stein's face was blank as he listened to my son's chest with a stethoscope. After a few moments, he nodded to the older nurse.

"So much pressure," Libby said in a low snarl. She squirmed in my arms with a strength that seemed impossible for her small frame. I held her still in a crushing grasp. She had to be numb from the chest down, but she was still vital.

"And here we have your second boy!" Abraham held up the infant in the same fashion as he'd done with the first baby. This baby didn't cry or make any sound like my first son had. The baby was given to the respiratory therapist named Henry. Dr. Potter joined Henry in his administrations. Still, no sound came from the limp baby.

In a monotone voice, Ida Morton said. "The bowel had been perforated."

"Bloody hell," Dr. Morton said under his breath. Abraham handed the pair suture material.

Abraham looked over the drape. "There's a complication, but it will be remedied momentarily. Libby's bowel has been nicked. Dr. Morton is suturing it now and then will test the closure. Once that is fixed, the peritoneal cavity will be flushed."

Small gurgling cries emanated from my second son. He wasn't as verbose as the first, but he wasn't blue anymore. *Thank God.*

Libby's lip trembled. It was hard to tell if she was in pain or just still scared.

"You're doing fine. Do you hear them? They've got your lungs." At least our first son had her lungs.

She gave way to a slight smile.

"Am I together yet?" Libby whispered. I looked over the drape, and Dr. Morton seemed to be finishing the internal sutures, though in all reality he was probably still fixing the bowel.

"Partly."

She balled her fists, and tears ran down her face.

"Kent!"

He was only a couple feet away.

"Yes, how's the patient?" The look in his eyes changed when he saw Libby's face.

In a lower tone than Libby could hear, I whispered to him. "She's panicking. Can you give her something to calm her nerves?"

Beyond Libby, the younger nurse shouted, "Dr. Potter, his Apgar is only three at five minutes!"

"I can, but it'll knock her out. Is that what she wants?" Kent's eyes danced from Libby and then back in my direction.

"It's what she needs. Please give it to her."

Kent nodded and added a cloudy liquid to Libby's IV line. Libby's fists slackened, and tension faded from her face. Dr. Morton finished suturing Libby thirty minutes after she'd fallen asleep. She couldn't have held out that long. The sedation was for the best. Libby was still connected to the heart monitor, respiratory, and pulse oximetry monitoring. Our nameless boys were alive. I prayed they'd both remain that way.

"Liam." I followed Abraham into my office, away from the medical team and the balance that everything seemed to hang on.

"You've noticed the difficulty that the second baby is having?"

My throat clinched, awaiting the dread to come. "Yes."

"Dr. Potter believes he has pneumonia." Abraham rested his hand on my shoulder. A storm of unkempt emotion threatened to explode, but I reined myself inward. Libby wouldn't be able to get over this, not losing a child.

"Give it to me straight. How long will he…last?" I gripped my desk, not wanting to fall on my face.

"He's weak—there's no doubting that, but we've caught it early. Dr. Potter is a leading neonatal pediatrician. I don't think we would have this hope without her. For now he'll be getting respiratory treatments, IV antibiotics, and will have to be tube fed. He's not out of the woods, but his odds are more than good."

I sighed. "That wasn't what I thought you'd say." I wiped wetness out of my eyes.

"Birth is rarely an easy venture."

Dr. Amy Potter knocked on the half-open door. Abraham waved her in. "Your second born is doing much better, Mr. O'Connell."

I shook my head at her formality. "Just call me Liam."

"Okay, Liam." She pushed back loose hair that had fallen from her ponytail. "Do you mind if I explain to you what's going on with your son?"

"Please."

"He seems to have congenital pneumonia. It can be a very serious condition, and would've in all likelihood taken your son's life without a quick diagnosis." She leaned against a filing cabinet. She emitted normal human smells in the midst of a vampire's den, and yet I was at her mercy. "He'll need IV antibiotics for the next week but shouldn't need any respiratory interventions for more than two to three days maximum. I'm going to insert a temporary feeding tube through his nose so he can still get nutrition. I'm afraid if we try and feed him orally at this point, he could aspirate more liquids into his lungs, which would only slow down his recovery. Do you agree with the treatment plan?"

I tried to follow along but was lost in her explanation. "Yes, please do whatever you need to do."

She nodded and turned to go back into the medical nightmare.

"Thank you," I said to her back.

An hour later I sat in a large chair that I'd brought down from the loft, my firstborn resting in my arms. I wanted solace for Libby so that it'd just be the three of us when she woke up. Our second born would be on constant observation until his lungs were clear and respiratory monitoring was no longer needed.

Her eyes fluttered and opened. "Are they okay?" Her voice was hoarse.

I nodded and situated our firstborn into her arms. "He's perfect."

Libby stared at the single bundle. "Where's our other baby?"

I sat down beside her on the bed. There wasn't much room, but I'd make it work. "He has pneumonia but is going to be fine."

"What?" Her brow knitted together, and her respirations intensified.

"Shhhh. I know it's scary, but he is going to be fine." Our first son jiggled in Libby's arms as she tried to keep herself from crying. She looked up through tear-strewn lashes. "Are you sure?"

"Apparently we have one of the top neonatal pediatricians available in Dr. Potter. I couldn't be more certain." Her breathing regulated as she caressed the cheek of the baby in her arms. She stared at our son's perfect face. He was unmarred and so innocent. She closed her eyes as if she was going back to sleep again.

"Do you want me to hold the baby?" I asked as Libby yawned.

"Not really, but it'd probably be safer if you did. Why am I so tired? I don't even remember anything after our second baby was born."

My stomach knotted. She had to know the truth. "I asked Kent to give you a sedative after the boys were delivered. I'm sorry."

"I guess that was for the best… Do they have all of their fingers and toes?"

I smiled. So I was forgiven. "Yes, all fingers and toes accounted for."

"What will we name them?"

"Whatever you want."

"Darcy and Pierce?" She smiled at me and looked back at the baby "This one will be Darcy. Pierce will be our fighter. He'll need a powerful name to get well."

"If that's what you want…they're fine names." Libby was waking more. Naming the boys was somehow revitalizing.

"That's what I want." The baby in my arms seemed hungry. He sucked on his fist before opening his mouth like a baby bird.

I kissed Libby's forehead. "I think he needs to feed."

"Where are the bottles?"

The expression she wore left no question as to how he'd be fed.

Bottles? "I don't know. I thought you'd breastfeed them."

Her expression iced over. "You'd better find the bottles and formula."

It was clear who the master of our relationship was. I did as she said.

After the baby fed, the solace disappeared. Grace, Shelby, Danny, and Abraham returned. The baby was passed around as I helped Libby to her feet. She didn't complain, but she grimaced as she moved.

How was this even possible? Our boys were miracles, and Libby a saint for enduring this pregnancy. I was beyond blessed.

***

Libby

Whoever said that motherhood changes your priorities was almost right. My priorities were more focused, like a sniper's aim. Gone were my apprehensions—there was no time left to waste. Darcy and Pierce were just over three days old and were almost identical, except for their size. Pierce was still on IV antibiotics but was breathing normally now and was as active as his brother. He was a fighter, just as I'd predicted. Liam doted on them and had changed every diaper and answered every cry. I wanted to do more for them, but Abraham limited my activity, saying I wouldn't recover if I didn't take it easy. Because of the bowel perforation, *of all things*, I had to take antibiotics four times a day. Doctor Morton would've preferred me on IV antibiotics, but I was done with IVs. I would've told him as much to his face, but Abraham smoothed it over with him first. So I'd listen to Abraham's advice and would spend a lot of time with a sleeping boy in my arms. I wouldn't overextend my body, being it hurt like hell to move as it was. Besides, I could get lost in the simple act of watching my boys sleep. It was too early to tell at this point, but their little noses looked like Liam's.

Abraham planned on staying around for a month more, but the other medical staff members would only be around a few more days. They had their own schedules to fulfill, and Abraham could manage us on his own. If there was a way to urge my dad to stay, I would, but it'd be impossible. My mom couldn't know the truth… Once again, he'd be gone.

Liam arranged the boys in their cribs as I hobbled to the bathroom to shower. I held a pillow over my incision to make walking more tolerable. Liam met me there and would help me bathe. I was so helpless, but I didn't want him to see that side of me. Not when I'd been so limited in the past months. It'd look like a pattern of weakness. For now I'd have to bear it, as healing had to be my priority. I stood on the cool tile as he heated the water and followed me in under the rain-shower faucet. Sex was off limits, as if I'd want it now anyway. Walking hurt, and sex was a lot more vigorous than that.

The soapy water washed over my incision. The water itself didn't cause pain, but nothing about recovery was pleasant. Liam washed me with the same attention he gave the boys. I leaned against him as the water rinsed off the remaining soap. He helped me out of the shower and patted me dry.

"The boys are doing so well…"

"All thanks to you." Liam held me in an oversized towel.

I bit my lip. He had to know what I wanted, right? "You know we need to talk?"

He brushed his cheek against mine. Maybe I should have waited until we were dressed? "I intend on marrying you, but don't you think that Shelby and Danny should have their wedding first?"

My God…this wasn't going to be easy. "That's not what I meant. I've thought about getting married, especially now that we have the boys, but…what about changing me first?" My pulse quickened. Couldn't he see how something as natural as pregnancy had affected me in the most negative of ways? I refuse to be weak when he has the power to change that for me.

"I thought you'd want time with the boys before you made any rash decisions. Maybe wait a year?"

"Holy hell, Liam. A year?" I shrugged out of his hold. Every day I remained human was one more day I aged. I couldn't escape time as a human, so waiting was out of the question.

"You don't know how it is to be a new vampire. You'll see the boys differently. You'll see me differently too." His voice was strained.

He didn't get it. Throughout my entire pregnancy, he'd seen me differently, but he couldn't see how it'd pained me all along. How could he see my point with his mind so set on keeping me human? I took a deep breath. I couldn't blame him for how he felt, no more than he could blame me for what had to be done. So I'd have to figure this out myself?

"Don't be angry. You're still recovering. You don't need more stress on your body."

"We'll talk about it another time." I walked into the bedroom as if my body had forgotten the healing it still had to do. I'd pay for that later. I pulled on a tunic and loose pants. I didn't care how I looked because…what did it matter? Nothing mattered when there was such an important issue unresolved. I wouldn't continue to age while he lived in eternal youth. I wouldn't be the only odd one out when my boyfriend, his brother, and my best friend all were vampires. It wasn't just, nor would I stand for it. Ignoring my plea was not an option. My life depended on it.

***

Liam didn't follow me when I told him that I was going to see my dad. He didn't understand…no, couldn't understand. How could he not see how impossible he was being? It was like asking me to stay a frog while he was the gorgeous prince.

I couldn't drive myself anywhere and could only get so far away. The ground was uneven, but I placed both of my hands over my throbbing incision, gritted my teeth, and plodded my way through the pine-needle-strewn yard. I thought the walk inside was difficult with abdominal surgery, but little did I know…

My dad's RV was nicer from the outside than the others. Price didn't seem to limit him, and it wasn't like he had anyone to support with the money that he pocketed. I knocked on the door and was greeted by his once familiar smile. This would be one of the last social calls we'd have before he was gone again. Turns out that both of the men in my life were simultaneously disappointing me. And I was the one who had relationship issues? *Yeah, right!*

The interior of the RV was nice. The style wasn't what I'd go for, but the sofa was leather, the flooring looked like Pergo, and the countertop could've been Corian.

I sat down on the sofa as Dad closed the door. I grimaced as I eased the pressure from my incision. Rage carried me here, but I'd be either carried or carted back home somehow. If I moved much more, my incision would likely rip open like a faulty shirt seam.

"You look great. How are you feeling?" My dad's smile warmed his face.

"I look like crap, but thanks anyway." I pushed my semi-wet hair behind my ears while trying to ignore the fact that I'd ruined any chance of my incision healing on its own accord. It wouldn't matter now anyway. "Actually, I came to collect a favor."

"And that is?"

His eyes focused on me. We were cut from the same material. I'd be blunt, since that was the language we best understood. "I want you to change me."

Silence filled the RV. He scratched his chin. "Are you serious about this? You realize that it'll change everything."

"I'm okay with that, Dad. It's what I want. It's been on my mind for a while, and I can't wait any longer." I dried my sweaty palms on my pants. He could say no, and there'd be nothing I could do about it.

"Have you asked, Liam? He'd want to know."

"He wants me to wait, but you know that he'll just keep pushing it off indefinitely. It has to be now. You have to do it." I sniffed back tears. My dad owed me this much.

Dad looked around the living room. "Are you sure about this? Blood will be your diet, and your babies won't have a human parent anymore." His eyes were panicked, but he seemed to be on my side.

"I know. I need this, Dad…" I widened my eyes and stared at him as he deliberated to himself.

"Why do you need this so badly, Libby? Help me to understand."

"I can't live disconnected like you did with Mom. I just can't!"

"You know that I loved your mother."

"Dad…that's not the point!" I pushed down my emotions the best I could. They'd only distract me from the issue at hand. "I don't want to be the fragile little girl that Liam has to tend to…I want, no…I need to be his equal. Can't you see? It's the only way any of this could work. He might think that he'll change me in the future, but the longer he waits, the less likely he'll go through with it. I don't only want this for myself. I need it…"

Dad was silent for what seemed like ages, though it couldn't have been for more than a few minutes. "Okay…I'll do it." He sounded uncertain, but I doubted he'd go back on his promise.

He looked me up and down.

"Now, Dad." The one thing I didn't have was time to waste. If Liam became suspicious or wanted to apologize for our disagreement, my plan would be ruined. I had to be changed before anything else got in the way.

Dad stood and locked the entry door. The windows were privacy coated except for the front cabin, which wasn't visible from the living room. "The change will hurt more than you can even imagine."

I nodded. "I don't care. This is what I want." If my pregnancy and caesarian birth hadn't already hardened me, then there'd be no way I'd ever be ready. His warning wouldn't dispel what needed to be done.

I followed him to the bedroom. He said that the pain would strike as soon as the change initiated, and I'd want to be somewhere comfortable. I took a deep breath, but my chest hammered away no matter what I did.

"You're sure?" Dad sat down beside me on the queen bed.

"Never more sure. What do I have to do?" My pulse pounded in my ears, making it hard to hear. This was scary, but I couldn't flinch and ruin my hardened facade.

He cleared his throat. Maybe he thought I'd change my mind? "You have to drink my blood. It doesn't take much."

Bile churned in my stomach. Somehow I heard him speak with more clarity than I thought possible despite the persistent whooshing in my ears. "Okay."

He pulled a small blade out of its sterile wrapper. I didn't want to see him cut himself, but I couldn't look away. He grazed his wrist, and dark blood dotted where the blade touched. Now all I could hear was loud static, like I was going to faint, but I reached for his arm. My vision darkened, but I tasted the metallic liquid on my tongue. My consciousness clawed its way out of darkness. The taste wasn't something I'd craved before, but now its tingle made me pull in more from the wound. He pulled his arm away as the room spun. This feeling was familiar and akin to being tipsy drunk. If my dad said anything more, I couldn't hear him. Swishing drowned out all other sounds. I dug into the bedding, but no matter what I did, I couldn't find my equilibrium. A wash of fire raked at my nerve endings. *Was I getting burned alive?*

***

Liam

Why did women think it was okay to storm out without resolving anything? Libby needed distance, and so did I. Grace would watch the boys while I got fresh air. The walls had a closing-in-on-themselves quality, but the night air was brisk and helped me to regain sanity. Grace would return to her own home in the morning. I'd celebrate once she was really gone.

She hadn't been that much of a pain and was helpful sometimes, but it was time for her to go. She was getting too *at home* in my house.

It was just after ten, but Danny wouldn't be asleep yet. I walked past the hum of RVs toward the dim path that led to Danny's. Soon it'd be quieter here, normal. The sounds of nature would no longer be drowned out by engines.

I let myself in through the basement door. Shelby looked up after draining the bag of blood she held.

"Where's Danny?"

Shelby licked a missed drop of blood from her lip.

"Showering. Why? Is something wrong?"

She'd warmed to me again, though it'd taken months. Libby's pregnancy rekindled our friendship in a way nothing else could've. I was no longer the unstable monster she feared would ruin her best friend.

I sat down on the old sofa. This wasn't the kind of confidence that could be shared while standing. Shelby followed my lead and sat down facing me.

"Libby's angry with me. You know that she wants to be changed."

A wry smile lit her face. "And she wants you to change her now?"

I nodded. Shelby knew Libby better than I did— they'd been friends since birth.

"She stopped talking to me about that months ago when I discouraged her. She doesn't really like criticism." Shelby scrunched her nose.

"She went to see her dad after I suggested putting it off a year." I thrust my fingers through my hair. It wasn't long but pushed itself in different angles that couldn't be tamed.

"If your idea doesn't match hers, she's not going to be happy."

"We're both that way. I, for one, am anything but happy right now. Would it kill her to push it off a little while longer? She doesn't have a clue what she's asking! You know what I mean."

"I do. Right now her main concern has to be the boys. They'll need their mom. Besides, it's hard to say how she'll react to the change."

"My point exactly!" At least someone around here could see reason.

Shelby's eyes glistened in the incandescent lighting. "Are you going to change her after the boys are a little older?"

Did I even have a plan? "I've thought about it a lot, and I'm still not one hundred percent certain. Libby thinks she wants this, but what if she's wrong? There'd be no going back." Ciara, or my imaginings of her, hadn't even known a solution, at least not with certainty.

"The worst part of it all is that there is no pressing need to change her. When Danny changed me, there wasn't another option. Libby's healthy and could wait a few more years. You could always change her after the boys are older, and she'd still be young."

"I wish she'd listen to us. She doesn't want to see reason."

I left Shelby's company when it was almost eleven. Libby had to be in bed by now. I took my shoes off at the entry, not wanting to disturb anyone's rest. I roused Grace from the reclining chair, her duty relieved. The boys were asleep in their cribs. Silent coos and snores assured their slumber. Libby's side of the bed remained empty. She was either still angry, which I didn't doubt, or she wanted more time with her dad, which was just as likely the case. I stripped and then climbed under the crisp sheets. She'd have her time with her father undisturbed. I owed her that much.

Pierce cried, waking Darcy. I eased up in bed. The clock read 5:38. Libby's spot was still absent. She was so infuriating when she wanted to be. I tended the boys. They'd slept longer than usual and were calmed with clean diapers. I wasn't quick at changing diapers, not with the onesies they wore. Their legs had to be funneled into their clothes one by one and then snapped all together. I fastened them into side-by-side swings and heated their bottles. The morning sunlight filtered through the windows by the time the boys were back in their cribs. Why on earth had Libby stayed away all night? We hadn't been apart that long since we'd first started dating. Weird. What point was she trying to prove? Maybe she thought I'd give in if she stayed away long enough.

Clanging and movement sounded from the living room. Grace was up and dragging her bags to the door. She shuffled with vitality that had been dormant during her stay. I closed the bedroom door behind me, not wanting the boys startled.

"Liam, help me with my bags. I hate to leave like this, but a friend of mine has had a heart attack. I'm meeting her at the hospital. I'm all she has."

I took her bags and placed them in her trunk as she followed me to the car. "I'll be by to see Libby and the boys sometime next week. Give Libby my love when she wakes up."

So Grace thought Libby was asleep, not absent.

"Will do." I shut her door, and she sped off down the driveway, her old burgundy car bouncing along the stone drive.

I eyed the Coachmen RV before going back inside.

Chapter 10

Deception

Libby

Time passed in the inferno I'd begged for. Was this why Liam wanted me to reconsider? My consciousness slipped in and out, but everything looked different from tear-hazed eyes. I thought I'd screamed all night long, but it could've been in my head the whole time.

"Libby, sweetheart…" My dad tried to rouse me. He didn't realize how alert I was. It was like lit matches peppered my body.

I moaned a wordless plea. I couldn't focus my eyes on my dad's face.

"I need to take you back to your house. Liam has to be worried." It all made sense now. The only reason my dad agreed to this was to appease me—he wouldn't have to wait it out as I made the change. Once again I'd be someone else's concern.

I turned my head, he couldn't… I had to finish this process first. Liam would hate me for this…

Without any further consultation, Dad scooped me into his arms and carried me to the house. The outside was cold, heaven. The sun blinded me as if it were a high-powered spotlight. None of it mattered though. My God, what had I done?

***

Liam

I held Pierce as Darcy swung. I could sooth one baby, but not both at the same time. I was outnumbered. A banging echoed from the front door. I snapped Pierce in his swing and turned it on so that he'd sway from side to side.

The banging grew louder, as if my door's frame would soon give way.

"Coming!"

Through the living room window, I could make out an odd outline of the loud visitor. I rushed to open the door. Kent stood holding a limp Libby. *My* Libby. Her head had fallen back as if she were boneless. I stepped back, giving Kent room to enter. This couldn't be...

"What did you do?" As if it wasn't obvious. The bastard didn't think. If only he'd never resurfaced.

He didn't answer.

Kent carried Libby to our bedroom and laid her down on the bed. Her hair was sweaty and her clothes wrinkled.

"What did you do?" I had to hear it for myself.

His silence filled in the words he wouldn't say.

"It's what she wanted. I'm sorry." Kent stepped back from the bed.

I dropped to Libby's side. Her eyes fluttered, and tears slid from the corners.

"I'll take care of her from here." My voice was as harsh. Kent turned and left without a fight.

I called Danny on my cell phone. He'd bring Shelby. I pulled off Libby's shirt and tugged down her pants. She was burning up. Shelby cried when she entered the bedroom. We'd tried to stop this from happening, but Libby was the most stubborn, most frustrating, most determined…

"Will you take care of the boys while I get her straight?"

Shelby nodded as she wiped away tears. Shelby moved the boys' gear out of the bedroom and then returned for the boys. Danny emptied the ice from the freezer into the tub and filled it with cold tap water. Danny ran back to his house to collect more ice. The scene was replayed and so similar to when Shelby had been changed.

"Damn it, Libby. Why did you have to do this?" I muttered. It didn't have to be like this, but that was all moot now.

At least it wouldn't be me she hated for making her into this.

Libby's body looked frail and bloodless. Her skin was pale, and her lips were blue edged. Her fingers trembled, and she cried in a whisper. Living this life and pushing through the pain was her punishment. Her cesarean scar was fading and would be gone as her body shifted from human to vampire. Her ribs were prominent, as were her hips. Just days before she was distended with pregnancy, and now there was little left of her. That was how the change was though…it burned away all remaining energy. Danny helped me to lift and lower her into the icy water. I hesitated when she yelped. Her pain cut through my anger like fangs.

"We've got to cool her off. You know she's burning up." Danny eased her legs all the way into the water. I did the same but braced her by her underarms to keep her head above water.

Abraham came in the bathroom with a bewildered look on his face. "Then it's true?"

I nodded.

Abraham's hand entered the water in search of a pulse. I'd seen him check her pulse countless times before. "Her heart rate is erratic, but that's to be expected."

"Is there anything you can give her?" Danny asked. He was thinking logically, while I was hoping to wake from this nightmare.

"Well, I could give her a narcotic, or we could ask Kent what he'd recommend."

"Whatever you have on hand will have to do. Kent's done enough already."

Minutes passed as Libby moaned and cried, tears meeting the cold water. Her breathing came more rapid as it verged on hyperventilation.

"Abraham!"

Danny helped me to lift Libby out of the bath. I carried her to the bed, where Abraham could get a better look.

Abraham unsheathed a hypodermic needle and injected it into Libby's arm. Seconds later she calmed. "It's a sedative used in psychiatric hospitals." He recapped the needle and listened to Libby's chest with his stethoscope.

With a towel, Danny dried the water trail that was left from the bathroom to the bed.

I squeezed Libby's limp hand, and she squeezed my hand back, or had I imagined it?

"Everything sounds as it should for now. She'll rest for a few hours, at the very least."

I cleared my throat but still sounded raw when I spoke. "Since her father is one of us..." I breathed out against the urge to scream at someone, tempering myself since Abraham didn't deserve that hostility. "Will it affect how she goes through the change?"

Abraham sighed. "I wish I had the answer to that, but this isn't something that's been documented. As you know, most paternal vampires leave their human partners, so it's too hard to say how it will affect the change." Abraham glanced over Libby's limp form. "It's going to be a rough couple days for her. She has so much repair work after the cesarean. The change acts like a clean sweeper and heals what needs to be healed, though as you know...the process is unforgiving."

I nodded, unable to speak. What Abraham said was true. The change wasn't kind or forgiving, but it healed all ailments in the end. This meant great pain in a normal, healthy body, and sheer havoc in a body weakened or compromised. This was one of the many reasons I wanted her to wait...she wasn't healthy enough to change. Not that she'd listened to me. *Hell would have an ice rink first.*

Abraham and Danny excused themselves, leaving me alone with Libby. I busied myself by stripping off her remaining wet undergarments. I moved her to the dry side of the bed and redressed her in light clothing. I brought in a basin of cool water and dipped a washcloth in it for her forehead. The change didn't have to be as terrible, not when I could take care of her.

***

Libby

My eyes didn't hurt anymore, as least not while they were closed. Reality was back but wavered, as if the image of it could still splinter into something sinister. I opened them to see Liam by my side. So he hadn't forsaken me after all? He looked haggard, even with perfect hair and smooth skin. My fingers trembled like an addict looking for my next high. I reached to touch him. He grabbed my hand and stilled its shaking. *What have I done?* There wasn't pain, but lament buzzed through every neuron, as if my synapses had been rewired.

"How are you feeling today?"

Good question. Liam wouldn't know what to say if I were honest. I'd forced myself into being a horrendous abomination. Instead I'd tell him my physical status. That'd be the only safe answer. "Dopey, I think." My words slurred. I sniffled back tears. I was embarrassing myself, and to what end? So I wouldn't age?

"It's not you. Abraham gave you an injection two hours ago. You've been getting them every four hours for the last three days."

I closed my eyes to the swirly, bright room. It seemed to intensify the longer I kept them open. "That's why everything looks and feels wrong." I spoke slow, enunciating every syllable to avoid further humiliation.

"You should be back to normal in a couple more hours." He pressed his lips to my forehead.

I tried to relax and let the sedating effect of the drug pull me back under…

Hours had passed according to the clock. My eyes flickered to adjust to the tamer lighting. I reached for Liam and squeezed his knee.

"Are you awake?"

The voice was familiar, but not Liam's. I turned to find Danny with my hand on his knee. I snatched it back. *What the hell?*

"I won't tell if you don't?" Danny said with a chuckle. "Liam! She's awake!"

"I didn't mean to do that." My heart thudded. I was more myself, or at least inside my own body, but still not quite right.

"Relax. I know you didn't." Danny left the room as Liam entered.

"You're really awake?" Liam looked strange, but then again, so had Danny. Their features more defined. Light glinted from my arm as I reached for Liam. So I looked different too? Light radiated off Liam like he was an archangel. I stared at his exquisite face until my stomach rumbled, breaking the spell. My throat dried in a way that was more uncomfortable than I'd ever remembered. Self-loathing could be abandoned for the time being. Feeding edged its way to the top of my hierarchy of needs. Everything else was trivial.

"I'm thirsty." My voice was dry and harsh.

"I'm sure you are."

How could I drink blood though? That reality wasn't something I wanted to face head on, but the dryness was almost too much to bear.

"Come on." Liam pulled me into a standing position. My step was lighter, more nimble. I pulled the hem of the short dress I wore—Danny turned his face away—as I had to see my scar. It wasn't hurting anymore. My fingers traced smooth skin, as if there hadn't been a scar to begin with.

"What about Darcy and Pierce?" I hadn't seen them in days. Not that I'd been awake or could've seen them, in any case.

"Whoa, now. You'll have to feed first. There's no other way around it."

I trailed Liam, while still in my bare feet, to his office, where he kept the blood. He'd said it was convenient and not a place visitors would wander into unattended. He had me turn around as he prepared the blood. He warmed it in a baby bottle warmer and handed me what looked like a cup I'd get from a drive-through. The straw was a thick green plastic. Anything that would hide its contents was welcomed. Soon enough I'd have to learn to feed without a crutch. A chill slithered up my spine.

"How do I?" I held the cardboard cup like it'd attack me.

"Like you would any other drink. I'll teach you to hunt, but for now let's take it one step at a time. Okay?" He sat back into his cushy office chair. He was so patient with me, and I didn't want to disappoint him.

I nodded, putting the straw to my lips. My stomach churned. This was when I'd gag or throw up.

I closed my eyes and took a small sip. The blood was like ice to my throat. It cooled and soothed in a way that shouldn't have been possible. The taste was neither good nor bad. I took another sip and had drained the cup within five minutes. I'd never labeled Liam as a monster, but there was no doubting what I'd become. I took to drinking blood without batting an eye. Wickedness was now stitched into my being.

"It's not as bad as I'd expected." Who knew that the blood would be the easy part of this?

"It usually works out that way." Liam pulled me into his lap. "Was this what you really wanted?" He looked like he wanted to say more, but didn't.

I nodded since there was nothing that could be undone. "It's different than I thought it'd be, but maybe that's a good thing." It was a good thing, right? My heart fluttered in panicked beats. I really couldn't go back now, not ever. I forced a normal breath. Liam had to be spared this panic. I'd done this to myself.

"You really scared me. It was like after Sam's attack. You were so limp. I hoped that Kent hadn't done something wrong." His expression was serious and hard to look at.

"I don't think he would've tried it on me if he didn't know what he was doing." Would he have? He hadn't been around as a father, so maybe he'd done it just to shut me up. Maybe that was where the doubt was coming from?

"That's beside the point. You went behind my back. I can't have that. We'll be together too long not to have a foundation of trust."

I looked away. He was right. "Just hear me out. You were scared to change me after what'd happened with Ciara. I get that. It couldn't have been easy. I thought that if I were changed without your permission, then you'd see that I'd never blame you." I looked back at his still-serious face, wishing I'd listened to him. But admitting that his first inclination had been right wasn't an option. I wanted nothing more than to be human again! But at the same time, I felt almost *compelled* to become like Liam, like…my dad.

"Yes, but if I wasn't in your life, then you wouldn't have known or wanted this kind of life."

"My dad was like you. Maybe it was something I was looking for all along but couldn't understand its pull until I met you."

"You have an answer for everything." He tapped his chin. "I need to know that you'll be honest with me in the future. No more loopholes. Can you promise me that?"

"I can, but can I expect the same from you?" Equality was all I wanted all along.

"Without a doubt."

That evening the RV processional began pulling away. My dad was the only one who hadn't left yet.

I was well fed but still had a chip on my shoulder that wouldn't abate. Liam was giving me space that I needed, but in that space outlandish thoughts fluttered. Since I'd awoken, my rationality was off kilter. I couldn't deny my part in what I'd become, but my dad had yet to explain himself. My nails dug into my palm. I couldn't push away the anger—

nothing I did seemed to alter its rage. Without any more silent deliberations, I went to my dad's RV.

The evening air was as crisp as when I'd gone there just days ago. The outside scents had changed, or maybe I was only able to really smell them now with senses that knew no limits. I didn't knock this time. There was no need for formality. Not with what I had to say.

My dad looked up from the sofa with his tablet in his lap as I slammed the door closed. It didn't slam with the drama that I'd intended.

He smiled as if I'd come on a social call. "You're looking great, sweetheart."

I grimaced. Sure, I'd probably never looked better, but what did that matter when everything was wrong? My heart accelerated again with its unfamiliar rhythm, its persistent throb thudding in my ears. I rubbed my temples. This had to stop. I hadn't noticed my dad move from his spot on the sofa, but when I opened my eyes he was standing by my side. He led me to the sofa, where I sat down without protest. My fingers trembled again like when I'd first woken up after the change.

"What's wrong?" Dad asked as he held my wrist over its pulse point.

"What do you think's wrong?" I wanted to scream, but my head already hurt, and that would only make the pain worse.

"Open your eyes."

I squinted until I could open my eyes all the way. He shone a small bright light into each eye.

"Damn it, Dad! That's not helping."

"I'm sorry." He clicked the flashlight and dropped it onto a nearby counter.

I watched him through narrowed slits. How could I trust him? I hardly knew him anymore.

"By any chance, were you given a sedative during your transition?" He ran his hand through sandy hair.

"If you were around, you'd know the answer already!"

He blinked once but didn't retort. "Do you really think I would've been welcome?"

"How could I tell? I was in agony."

He flinched as if I'd thrown a blow. "I only did what you asked me to do."

"How could I know what I was asking?" I sat back against the sofa cushion. My head still throbbed, and now I was getting dizzy.

"You never answered my question." His voice was stern, fatherlike. He was letting me know who the parent was.

"Abraham gave me something every few hours while I transitioned."

"Okay, that makes sense then. Sometimes when you come off of a powerful sedative, it can have side effects, especially if they're not tapered."

I sniffled. My emotions were like a hurricane, occasionally settling in the eye but then twirling in the force of the winds again without warning. "What does that even mean?"

He took one of my hands and gave it a little squeeze. "It means that you'll need another dose and will need to be gradually taken off the drug. Don't worry. It will only take a day or two to get you off the drug completely."

"Does this make me an addict?"

"No, not at all. It makes you a living being, even if you are virtually indestructible."

I would've laughed, but my head threatened to implode.

When I awoke just forty-eight hours later, my sanity had returned. I thought I was normal, but I couldn't have been more wrong. Gone were the irrational regret and blame I first harbored. It didn't even make sense anymore. This existence was what I'd wanted. My fingers no longer trembled, nor did my head ache. Liam was my anchor, and I couldn't begin to fathom how gorgeous he was. I mean, he was hot when I was a human, but now... *Damn!*

My dad stayed by my side while I recovered. Liam guarded him like a convict, and I doubted that he'd ever trust my dad again. My dad donned a face mask when Mom visited me—she'd been told that I had a virus. It was hard to ignore the stolen glances Dad took in of Mom. So he really had loved her on some level. Maybe he always would.

As much as I didn't want this utopia to change, my dad had to move on to his next assignment. He'd spent the last hour packing up his equipment and was now readying to leave.

He'd come back inside to say good-bye.

I threw my arms around him. It felt like a part of me was being taken away. *Again...*

"You'll see me again, sweetheart."

"Where are you headed to this time?" Now that I understood the truth, it was a little easier to swallow.

"New Mexico. I don't have to be there until the week after next, but it's a long drive. It'll give me time to acclimate myself there." Dad talked all while continuing to hold me.

"You'll call and come to see me?" My voice cracked.

"Of course I will. I'll want to see my grandsons grow up, and maybe my daughter get married?"

"I'd like that too, Dad."

He pulled away with tears in his eyelashes. Dad patted Liam on the back as he went to the door.

Liam's stance was rigid. He wouldn't forget my dad's intervening, even though it was my will that pushed him to change me.

With the caravan out of sight, the house and property was quieter. Abraham still milled about, but I was used to having him around. It might even be harder to say good-bye to Abraham than it had been to watch my dad leave. The boys were temporarily staying with Shelby and Danny. My mom couldn't keep up with two infants, which was just as well. She was back home, so it wasn't likely she would've even noticed my transformation. It was easier having the boys at another house for now, just to be safe. I didn't think I'd hurt them, but what if I did? I'd seen them and held them under supervision, but being alone with them wasn't an option…yet.

***

"You're not going to wear that, are you?" Liam pulled the loose fabric of my bridesmaid's dress. I'd bought it when I was pregnant, but my body was so different now. I couldn't have predicted how recovered I'd be this soon after having the boys. If I were still human, the dress might have fit. Heck, it would've probably been too snug. Now that it was Shelby and Danny's wedding day, finding a new dress was out of the question.

"I don't see how I can." I turned side to side in front of the mirror. It wasn't flattering at all.

Liam went to the closet and came back with a garment bag. It hadn't caught my eye hanging in the closet, being it had been mixed in with Liam's clothes. He unzipped the black cloth bag and slid out a holly berry–red strapless, fitted cocktail dress. The color matched the dress I had on. So he had a contingency plan?

"When did you buy this?"

"When the wedding colors were picked. There was always a possibility that you'd be a vampire by now, and I didn't want you to miss out on Shelby's big day."

"It's perfect. Thank you." I threw the baggy dress on the bed and shimmied into the new upgraded one. I stood still as Liam zipped the back.

"It fits you perfectly." He pulled me to his side and kissed me. His facial hair rasped my lips. He made a faint growling noise that halted me… We had to get to the wedding though. I slid on black high heels, and we each grabbed a baby. I'd put bibs on the boys over their baby-blue tuxedos but would pull them off before the ceremony. Both boys were back under our roof now. We'd all worried as to how I'd react around them, but I soon realized I wouldn't harm them. My heart ached for the boys in a way that thrilled my senses. Never would I have guessed that motherhood had such perks. Even with Darcy's colic and Pierce's inability to sleep through the night, they were safe. They still seemed like they were a part of me, just without the bother of having umbilical cords.

The lawn was heavy with cars parked in every empty spot. There were so many cars that some trailed the sides of the main road, and some were parked on a bald field across from Danny's property.

Janice had fought to have the ceremony in her church, but Shelby convinced her that if they rented a tent, the guest list could be unlimited. The tent was large enough to fit up to 250 guests. It was situated at the bank of the river and was warm despite the December chill. White tulle covered the tent's ceiling along with strings of white lights. Electricity was powered by portable generators, and heaters occupied every corner. Both the ceremony and reception would happen in the tent, which was good since it was in the forties outside.

My mom attended to the boys as Liam and I stood with Danny and Shelby. They exchanged their vows, both looking sure of their union. The majority of the guests were human, which meant they couldn't understand how permanent our marriages were.

Shelby's dress was fitted at the top in a corset style with a large belled-out bottom. She'd taken my advice and went for the most garish dress she could find. She looked like a brunette Cinderella, but a thousand times more memorable.

After the ceremony, the guests were served appetizers as the pictures were taken. Shelby and Danny opted for outdoors photos. It was chilly, but none of us were affected by the weather. Instead of going back into the tent, Liam ushered me to the house. A refueling was needed to keep both of our cravings at bay. I still couldn't hunt, nor did I want to. The blood was tolerable and filling, but alfresco wasn't something I needed to experience just yet. Liam prepared two bags for me, while he only needed one. He still warmed the blood for me—cold blood wasn't appetizing. Once finished, I checked my makeup in the bathroom mirror. Liam's hands wrapped around me from behind. I jumped, knocking myself back into his hold.

"You're dazzling tonight."

He trailed kisses from my earlobe down to my shoulder. I'd been ready to go back to the reception, but the fuse had been lit by his close proximity. We hadn't made love since the boys were born, and most of that was because I'd been scared. If I were still human, I'd have to restrict sex until six weeks after delivery. This body didn't require restrictions…

I turned in his arms to face him. Liam's hazel eyes appraised me. All fears and apprehensions were gone. He kissed me and held my face between his hands. I couldn't get away if I'd wanted to, not that I wanted out of his grasp.

"I've missed this," I muttered between kisses. He lifted me onto the bathroom vanity, my legs wrapped around his waist. Fabric kept us from one another, but it wouldn't for long. He lifted me and carried me to our bedroom and set me down by our bed. The house was quiet. Finally alone.

I offered my back to him so that he could unzip my dress. The silky-red fabric slid to the floor. I turned to face him in my black strapless bra and matching panties. He peeled off his tuxedo, one article of clothing at a time. A pulsating stir surged through me… I needed him. He stopped undressing once he was down to his gray geometric-patterned boxer-briefs. The soft fabric hugged his body. Liam pulled me onto the bed. He unhooked my bra and slid my panties down. He pulled my nipple into his mouth. His mouth was rough—he didn't have to hold back anymore. I arched my back, pushing toward him as he took in my other nipple. *Why did we wait for this?* He pulled off his underwear and flipped me so that I was on top of him. I closed my eyes against the strange new sensations. He held my hips to match his rhythm.

"Oh!" I braced my hands on the mattress, and he took my breast in his mouth again. *What was he doing to me?* A scorching intensity grew between my legs. I pushed down on him as my body spasmed and flashes of red and pink lit up inside my closed eyes. My body flailed, but he pulled me flush to his chest. Just when I thought my orgasm was finished, he bit me. Pleasure reignited, causing me to shudder against him. He climaxed too as he thrust without abandon. I lay atop him motionless and without uttering a sound for minutes after. He finally took the initiative and laid me by his side.

"Was that okay?" Liam caressed my shoulder.

"Are you serious? You made me lose my mind. I didn't know it could be like that." My voice was weak from exertion.

He smiled. "The bite wasn't too much?"

"No, it was amazing."

"We've got to get back to the party, you know?"

Could I even move? "They won't miss us."

Liam furrowed his brow. "You know they will."

"Fine…" I rolled off the bed with poise that shouldn't have been possible after what we'd done. Liam helped me back into the dress, and I fixed my makeup and hair as he redressed himself. My hair still looked good—the hair spray could've held an airplane in the air. My lipstick was smeared but didn't take long to fix it.

When we stepped back into the tent, it looked like a rave. Even Shelby's grandmother was on the dance floor. Abraham's red hair caught my eye. He was dancing with a big-breasted brunette. He displayed energy that didn't seem possible, while his partner was doing her best to keep up with him. He'd be leaving tomorrow. I wasn't ready for him to go, but he had another patient to attend in Colorado.

Shelby pulled me to the dance floor. For once I didn't have to force her to move her body. She shook and shimmied like she'd been born to dance. I moved my hips, delighting in the most awesome wedding reception yet.

***

Liam

I took Abraham and Libby to the YMCA. Abraham liked to get his blood pumping, and something about being a vampire made us exceptional swimmers. Abraham was leaving us this afternoon, and I thought it'd be nice to share a memory before he left us for good. For once we could do something together without anyone's life being in the balance. I loaned him a pair of swimming trunks. That was the one thing he hadn't packed.

We three stood at the edge of the pool in front of divided swimming lanes. "On your mark. Get set. Go!" Abraham and I dived in head first, while Libby jumped into her lane like a kid, feet first. I pushed through the water. It was as smooth and unresisting as air. I turned under once at the end of the lane to return to the start. Abraham matched my pace, while Libby was still yards behind. I touched the pool's side in victory.

"You're good," Abraham said. He was a little breathless but not deterred.

"You're not bad either." I pushed myself back up onto the cement.

"How do you do that?" Libby shrugged with her hands facing upward on each side.

"You'll get better with practice. Do you know how to dive?"

"I never had swimming lessons," Libby said.

"I taught myself. It gets easier." Abraham dried his face with a towel.

"I was faster than I'd ever been, but don't know the proper techniques," Libby said.

"Don't worry. I'll work with you." That wasn't the only thing I planned on practicing with her.

We stayed for almost two hours but finally had to head home, as Abraham needed to get to the airport. If we were human, we'd prepare him a going-away meal, but that would've been disgusting, considering our diet.

Grace was at our house with the boys. She didn't mind dropping by to spend time with them. She was beginning to grow on me…a little. Danny and Shelby came over to see Abraham off, and Danny volunteered to drive him to the airport.

Danny and Shelby would be leaving in a few days too, Fiji bound. I'd drive them to meet that flight.

Abraham hugged Libby. "This has been an unexpected journey. Look at you now—more vital than I could've imagined when we first met."

Libby blushed. Since Grace was in the living room, not much more could be said about how huge the change really had been.

"It's going to be so weird without you. It's like you're a part of the family now."

She wasn't wrong. He'd swooped in and saved Libby. She'd be dead without his intervention. He was akin to an honorary brother now. "You'll come back and visit us, won't you? I know you have to get some downtime. Our door's always open." I pulled Libby to my side and shook Abraham's hand with my spare arm.

"I'd be honored. I'll call when I get a break. I'd love to go to the beach sometime."

"It can get rough, though I'm sure the waves won't slow you down."

"Probably not." Abraham nodded once more to Libby and was off.

Libby dried her eyes. She'd miss him too.

Shelby held Pierce in the large La-Z-Boy and fed him a bottle. Grace was in the other La-Z-Boy with Darcy, who'd fallen asleep. Libby pulled me back toward the front door. The boys were best left undisturbed.

Tomorrow Libby was returning to work part time. Her boss practically begged her to come back. She seemed to love the work, so it'd be good for her to get out of the house. She'd only be in the office three days a week, and a combination of Shelby, Grace, and I would watch the boys while she worked.

We meandered through the backyard. The tent was still up and would be picked up sometime during the week. We walked through the vacant tent. It seemed soulless without the crowd that had occupied it less than twenty-four hours before.

"Would you like a big event like Shelby and Danny had?" Libby sounded detached, but that was a trick she used to mask deeper emotions.

"I'd like you to choose that. It can be just you and me, or the whole city can come if that's what you want. I'm flexible."

"I vote destination wedding. I plan and design things all the time. I'm ready for whimsy." She stopped in the middle of the dance floor. I took her right hand and placed her left hand over my shoulder. I moved in the basic box step. She followed my lead without music.

"When would you like to get married?" I'd been a married man for most of my existence. I'd like that commitment again, but we had time.

"I'm not in a rush. At least not for a formal affair."

She looked over my shoulder before meeting my eyes. "I want the boys to be a real part of it too. We could always get our marriage certificate at the courthouse and have the real ceremony when the boys are two or three."

I leaned in to press my cheek against hers and swayed with her body. She had elegance like no other. "That's perfect." I cleared my throat. "I love you."

She batted her lashes. "You know that I love you too." I brushed my whiskers across her lips. She surprised me with a kiss and then turned my head to the side. The prickle of her fangs drew blood. She giggled into my ear.

"What was that?" I wiped away the trace of blood that lingered on my neck.

She whispered. "Next time we're…together, it's my turn to bite."

My blood pulsated. What an interesting idea… "Don't make promises you can't keep."

"That's not my intention. You just wait…"

THE END

About the Author

Kari nearly faints at the sight of blood, so after ten years of nursing, she said good-bye to her patients and turned to her true passion—creating stories. She writes full time, and since she took the leap, she's never looked back. Because that would make her dizzy.

If you love the book, you can join here to sign up for updates at:

http://karialice.com/

Please consider leaving a review at Amazon and

Goodreads.